Folktales

from

South Sudan

Retold by
David Aoloch Bion

The publisher wishes to acknowledge and thank Dr Douglas H. Johnson for his invaluable help and support for Africa World Books and its mission of preserving and promoting African cultural and literary traditions and history. Dr Johnson and fellow historians have been instrumental in ensuring that African people remain connected to their past and their identity. Africa World Books is proud to carry on this mission.

ISBN: 9780645398816

Cover design, typesetting and layout: Africa World Books

Contents

Chapter Two

Chapter Three

Introduction

C hoosing a title that substantially reflects the essence of the stories in this book has not been an easy job. Are they legends, myths, folktales, folklores, fables, legends, fairy tales or what? To a large extent, one would say each of these tales can qualify to take nearly any of the possible titles listed above. But that raises the question: are all these words synonymous-meaning, do they share the same meaning? The answer is a definite no because they are, strictly speaking, not identical despite their similarity in meaning. If so, which word or words will accurately reflect, as much as possible, the category of all these stories? Arbitrarily, it was decided as a matter of convenience, to categorise the stories as fables and folklore. The reader is free to agree or disagree with my decision when they reach for the stories.

Usually, a problem of this nature is resolved by resorting to a dictionary to arbitrate. For our purpose, I have resorted to the Oxford English Dictionary to assist us in clarifying the words that have been chosen for the title. The first is 'folktale' (for the dictionary it is written as two words- folk tale). The dictionary says, a folk tale is "a very old traditional story from a particular place that was originally passed on to people in a spoken form." Since most of the stories in this collection meet the three criteria, namely: being traditional, from a particular place and having existed orally until the time the narrator finished writing them down in English, 'folktales' surely beats the rest for the title choice.

Another aspect of folktales, sometimes known as fables, is that animals such as a fox or hyena, birds and so forth, play a central role in these stories, as they do things that humans do, mainly action and speech. In most of the stories in this book animals play leading roles.

The other stories- recent in origin- can come under the 'folklore' rubric because, unlike myths, which are usually understood to refer to ancient times, they may not always be time-specific. Again, the Oxford Dictionary online defines folklore as "the traditions and stories of a country or community." Irish or African folklore as an example, adding that, "the story became part of the family folklore."

Another point that requires clarification is the title, *Folktales from South Sudan*. The impression readers may form is that the stories have been drawn from the various cultural and nations (ethnic groups) that live in South Sudan, the nation state that became independent in 2011. According to official estimates, that African country is made of up of 64 nationalities (or 'tribes' according to many people especially among South Sudanese themselves). This figure is based on grouping people on the basis of a common language, a criterion can be grossly misleading since speakers of mutually intelligible dialects- for example, the Kuku of Kajo Keji and the Kakwa of Yei, both in Central Equatoria, or the Agaar speaking Dinka of Rumbek in Lakes State, and the Dinka Malual of Aweil in the Bahr el Ghazal region, are treated as separate tribes. Members of a nation or nationality usually share a common tongue while its constituent members speak different dialects of that language that are mutually intelligible. That type of classification-counting speakers of dialects instead of those who share a common language, gives South Sudan more ethnic communities than the exact numbers on the ground.

The narrator of the folktales in this book speaks and writes in one of the many Dinka dialects as his first tongue. Some of these stories- mainly the fables-exist in other dialects of the Dinka, in unknown numbers. Innumerable stories remain unwritten either in Dinka or in any of the other languages of South Sudan. These stories face being lost for ever as urbanisation is gradually doing away with the tradition of story telling by rural folks around a fireside at night.

On the basis of the preceding note, it would have been fitting to narrow the scope of the tales by describing them as Dinka fables and folktales rather than labelling them folktales of South Sudan. Well, giving the stories a broader berth does no harm; after all Dinka people live in South Sudan.

Having tackled the problem of nomenclature we can now take a glance at the possible origins of ancient tales.

It is probable that as soon as members of early human communities began to communicate with each other by means of speech, singing and storytelling was included. But the problem was stories that existed in spoken form saw them undergo continuous change in content and format as a result of retelling them.

That problem was solved many years after writing became part of enduring communication forms, when the literary value of those stories was recognised in Africa (Ancient Egypt and Ethiopia), Middle East, Asia, and Europe, where the process of committing the tales to written form began. In time, the rest of the world began to share those treasures. Among those were the fables that are attributed to a Greek story-teller, Aesop, (although some scholars doubt his existence), the Mesopotamian *Epic of Gilgamesh, Alef Leila wa Leila* (*One Thousand and One Nights* in Arabic), and many others.

Folktales, particularly the legends and myths of creation, have existed since the time humans began to live in communities. Speech played an important part, not only as a medium of interpersonal communication, but also as a tool for entertainment such as singing and storytelling. It is possible to deduce that our ancestors spent their time, telling fables around fire hearths or in their mud huts before they slept. The stories were passed on to the next generation until our own time.

With such a history of retelling over time, those old stories underwent changes. If one were to lay hands on what could be considered as a prototypical myth or legend- if ever there is such a thing- its latest adaptation would be seen to have almost nothing to do with the first version.

It can be stated with certainty that since fables, myths and similar stories are so widespread all over the world, it may be fair to believe that nearly every cultural and linguistic community today must have its own trove of ancient tales.

Unlike their counterparts from the rest of the world, the written form of ancestral stories from Africa can be considered as some of the latest arrivals on the literacy scene. It was about the 19th century when Western Christian missionaries and anthropologists began to collect ancient, oral tales from their African hosts. When those pioneering folklorists had learned to speak and write the languages of their hosts, they then transcribed the fables, translating those African tales into their native European languages, mainly English, French, or Portuguese.

In the last century, Sudanese students, (including those from southern Sudan), read the most famous folktales in Arabic. Although a few of them were to be found in English textbooks which used fables for teaching comprehension and building vocabulary.

Reverand Archibald Shaw, a British member of the the Church Missionary Society (CMS) and known to the Dinka as Macuor, helped establish Malek station in 1905, as a centre for evangelism, and later to become an elementary school. In 1918, Rev. Shaw published

Dinka folktales in the journal, *Sudan Notes and Records*.
The journal, which was published in Khartoum, carried writings on nearly every aspect of the country from archaeology and ethnology through to zoology. Rev. Shaw had learned and used the Bor dialect of Dinka to translate the gospel of Luke before the fables in Dinka. At that time the Dinka orthography was in its infancy, (for example diphthongs representing /ny/, /dh/, /nh/ were represented by a single phoneme) with a diacritic beneath or above it, while /ŋ/ (/ng/) in its present form had a different sign in the form of /n/.

The Dinka versions of the stories ran alongside their English counterparts. Those folktales were collected from the village people who narrated them and were later checked by schoolboys at Malek. The stories became part of the curriculum in the verrnacular at the time.

Other traditional stories of note from Dinka are those retold in *Dinka Folktales: African Stories from the Sudan*, which were published in 1971 in the USA, by Dr Francis Mading Deng, polymath and writer of many acclaimed books on several subjects. The publication of the book coincided with the decade following the incorporation of traditional African stories, especially the myths of creation, into mainstream literary works by African novelists and poets – spearheaded by the British publishing company, Heinemann under its African Writers Series.

One of the first books of this series to be published was Taban lo Liyong's *Eating Chiefs from Lolwe to Malkal*. Those tales were described as "a collection of myths and ancestral stories from Uganda and East Africa." Taban lo Liyong prefers 'transmuted' to 'retold,' by which he means that the old story is not only being narrated as received; it is also being remade.

Ulli Beier, the German born academic, developed interest in the Yoruba fables when he was teaching in Nigeria. With the assistance of Yoruba speakers, he became instrumental in producing a substantial amount of written literature out of the traditional Yoruba folk stories. Among those are *Origin of Life and Death: African Creation Myths* and *Not Even God is Ripe Enough* (co-authored with Bakare Gbadamosi, a Nigerian).

With a few exceptions, fables, or other forms of traditional stories, do not have known authors; communities are presumed to be their inventors, while those people who collect and compile them should be referred to as retellers. The origins of mythologies, which are part of folktales, can be found in attempts by old societies to explain the mysteries of the world in which their members inhabited. The objective of the legends were to understand and explain life puzzles such as creation, death and life after death, or spiritual beings and their relationship with humans.

Then there is the obvious question: what is the value of these ancient stories, most of which strike the hearer or reader as illogical and out of tune with the modern world of science in which things or ideas that do not satisfy rational scrutiny are readily dismissed as ridiculous?

There are four possible reasons to account for the un-dimished attraction legends, folktales, fables, and myths (of creation for example) still have in the modern world.

First, fables, legends, and myths are valued as part of a cultural heritage that gives us an idea of how our very distant ancestors lived and their view of the natural world, how they could explain it, and their place in that scheme of things. In other words, these stories take us to explore the ancient world, its prevailing belief systems and their knowledge of the physical world at the time.

Second, for thousands of years societies have used fables as a vehicle for passing on lessons in morality: bad behaviour is punished, while wise and correct acts are praiseworthy. In the introduction to, *A First Book of Fairy Tales*, retold by Mary Hoffman, she says: "All over the world, tales were handed down from generation to generation. Many fairy tales shared the same themes- good always triumphed over evil, and the central characters lived happily ever after." In short, the tales served as lessons in morality.

Aesop's Fables contain stories that point in that direction as is shown by many maxims drawn out of them. Among these are: "unity is strength" (from the story of the man and his sons who used to quarrel among themselves, and the bundle of sticks), or "the slow but steady wins the race" (the race between the tortoise and the hare).

Third, back in time when fables were used for entertainment, storytelling played the role we now assign to movies, books, works of arts or recorded music during leisure time.

Finally, recalling old times can generate nostalgia in people. Anyone recalling happy school days will not miss some of the books or stories one read in class. Reliving such memories can sometimes be pleasant. In their book, *Folk Tales and Fables of the World,* Barbara Hayes and Robert Ingpen write: "They [folktales and fables] appeal to all ages, from young children, who will revel in having these stories read to them, to parents and grandparents, for whom they will revive memories of childhood."

There is need for a word to be said about the format

and style of the stories one will be reading shortly. As you read through the fables and folktales in this book, it will become clear, if readers are familiar with folktales from around the world, that these are different in that most of them are much longer than say, Aesop's, for example. In that respect they can be likened to the German Grimm Brothers' *Fairy Tales*. That should not discourage a potential reader; Grimms's fairy tales are interesting despite being long. What matters most is how the stories are told. For the stories in this collection, the narrator has employed a tantalising suspense as a means of asking: what will happen next? This technique has rendered the stories fascinating and worthwhile as it holds the reader captive.

The problem for the reader may revolve around the idiom in the original medium. Like any other language, Dinka has idioms, which when translated into any other language and taken literally, would be a hodgepodge of words, signifying little or nothing at all to a non-Dinka speaker. One such expression is, "wife of my Father's cattle," a literal translation of "*tiŋ de yɔ̈k ke awä/wää*," is a sheer absurdity when taken literally. To make sense out of this apparent nonsense, what the statement means is that a man is addressing the wife he married after giving a herd of cattle- in form of bride wealth- owned by his Father to the family of his wife.

This clumsy expression is put simply as "my lovely wife." There were several problematic expressions in the book, but their nearest equivalents in English have been adopted instead. One such example is: "he almost vomited intestines out..." or "*acï cïin duɔr ŋɔk*" in Dinka. The context in which this kind of expression is used is in reference to a character in the story having ingested poison- deliberately but covertly served to him. It can also imply shock: when the character learns the meat, he has consumed happens to be the flesh of his own child. In this translation, the idiom reads, "he vomited severely..."

Another idiom, "Personality ox (or bull)," deserves to be explained here in full. Made famous by Francis Mading Deng, (mentioned above), this is a nickname the Dinka people use to attach to individuals. An ox or a bull, is dedicated to a man, often after initiation into manhood. Such a nickname becomes part of his personal identity. The person so named, would invoke the nickname based on different physical attributes, mainly the colour configuration of the ox. In the patrichial Dinka society of the past, women were mostly denied a nickname; very few of them would get such an honour, the exceptions were rare indeed.

One of the favourite personality ox sobriquets is Majok (Majök)- white with black spots around the neck or face and neck. Colours, their shades and mode of their distribution over the animal, as well as the style and shape in which humans manipulate the horns to permanently bend towards a desired direction, all contribute to the grace for which an ox becomes a symbol of the adulation that is normally reserved for an icon.

It is in that regard, in the fable in which Awan the Fox is fond of "Riardien-ci- riar-wen" (*Riardien-cï-riar-awën*), 'Riar' is a suffix indicating the colour of an ox-the configuration of white and black. This ox is known as Marial or Mariar, depending on the dialect used. In provoking the nickname of his personality ox, the Fox is expressing his displeasure with someone else over an issue on which the two disagree. In plain language this utterance is understood to mean, "How dare you do or say such a thing to me!"

Away from belligerence, a personality ox moniker can be invoked to express what amounts to self-praise and glorification. An example of this happens when a person throws a weapon at an object, such as an animal being hunted. When the spear hits the target, the person who has hurled it jumps up in a celebratory mood while loudly shouting the attributes of their personality ox. This self-congratulatory act is what Okot p'Bitek, the Ugandan writer, calls '*moch*' in Acholi language. The Dinka versions are: *miöc, möc, guak, waar*, and the like, depending on the dialect the person speaks.

A non-Dinka speaker will also come across expressions such as 'horned cow' or 'hornless cow' repeatedly. In other cultures, a cow may simply be a cow, but in traditional Dinka culture a cow is actually a pervasive and complex form of obsession. Long-horned cattle, especially when the horns are gnarled, are highly treasured, while those with short horns or without them are graded as less valuable aesthetically speaking.

A few Dinka words that are maintained in the stories are explained at as footnotes or in the glossary at the end of the story. They have been reduced to a minimum so as not to distract the reader.

To conclude this introduction, it necessary to remind the reader that fables and folktales are an important aspect of the cultures of the people of South Sudan. Many, many of them remain undocumented and if nothing is done in the short term to capture them right now, most of them will be lost with the passage of time.

Efforts such as this one, by David Aoloch Bion, should be appreciated and encouraged as part of our collective responsibility to preserve and promote our cultural heritage. It is my humbles hope that a body of volunteers devoted to collecting and recording of fables and folktales from *all* the various cultural and linguistic groups in South Sudan in an alphabetical order A to Z (from Acholi to Zande) should be created by members of the communities who speak and write those languages of the 64 nationalities, or whatever figure one believes to be the exact number of tongues we speak as individuals or communities.

There is no reason why we cannot work to promote our diverse and rich cultures since we are no longer under the rule from Khartoum, which deliberately promoted Arabo-Islamic cultures over our African heritage and ways of life judged primitive and decadent by the former Sudan's ruling class. There is nothing wrong with them; they are part of our identity as a people. South Sudanese should take pride in their diverse and rich cultures.

[Atem Yaak Atem's Dinka translation of a selection of Aesop's Fables, Akëkööl Thɛɛr ke Ayethop, was published in 2018. Illustrations were made by the renowned South Sudanese cartoonist, Adija Achuil]

Chapter 1

Fox's Egg

O nce upon a time, Awan, the Fox, also known as Adukuäu, visited Nyang, the Crocodile, his maternal aunt. Nyang lived across the river. It was dry season, and therefore a lean time when there was a food shortage. Awan arrived at Nyang's home in the evening. Nyang was not happy because he did not have food to give to Awan as there was famine in the land. Nyang was forced to eat tubers, berries and the leaves of some trees and plants. Nyang pleaded with Awan to eat what was available until better days to come. That evening Awan fed on food made from tubers.

The following morning, Nyang and Awan went to collect wild fruits and tubers around the ponds in the nearby forest. On returning home in the evening, Nyang told Awan to prepare a meal in the house that was partitioned in two, big and small parts, with the wall between them. Nyang cooked in the small part of the house. In the larger section, Nyang had laid ten eggs, which were in a circular sandy cage.

While he was cooking Awan stole an egg from the nursery. He pierced the egg to make a small opening on it, then he poured the yolk into his food. Having done that, he carefully sealed the shell as if it had never been broken. He then returned the shell to the remaining nine eggs in the nest.

When Nyang and Awan had finished cooking, they sat down for their evening meal.

As they were eating, Nyang noticed some pleasant scent wafting from Awan's calabash dish, indicative of a delicious meal. Surprised by what she was smelling from Awan's meal, Nyang asked him: "My nephew, why is this mouth-watering scent wafting from your meal? What did you add to the leaves I gave you?"

"I do not know, my aunt," Awan replied.

"Can I taste your food?" Nyang requested Awan.

Awan scooped a seashell spoonful from his dish and gave it to Nyang to eat.

"It is delicious. How do you cook it?" Nyang wondered.

"I wash my hands clean, and I place what I cook on it," Awan said.

On another day Nyang and Awan went to pluck the leaves and creepers from shrubbery and along the shore. When they returned home in the evening, Nyang washed her hands clean, placed them on her food, according to Awan's advice. While on the other side of the wall, Awan picked another egg, poured the yolk into his food, and returned the shell to the cage. When they came out to eat, Awan's food released an appetising scent unlike Nyang's dish.

"My nephew, Awan," Nyang stated, "I have washed my hands clean, and I placed them on the food. But my food still is not as delicious as yours. Can you explain?" Nyang wanted to know.

"I do not know, my aunt," Awan replied.

That evening Nyang left the matter there and did not ask anymore about the dishes containing the food made from the same stuff that had a different taste and scent. Despite the mystery of the food's origin, Nyang happily lived with Awan for nine days. During that time, Awan continued stealing the eggs from the cage, one every day, which he used for his food. During those days, Awan had emptied the eggs of yolk in them. On the other hand, Nyang would visit the part of the house where the nursery was. During each of those visits Nyang did not see anything wrong since all the ten eggs were in the cage as usual. At the time when there was only one egg with a yolk left, Awan told Nyang he wanted to leave.

"I am happy that you came to see me, my nephew," Nyang told Awan.

"What gift shall I be taking with me since now I am returning home?" Awan asked.

"As you have seen with your own eyes, my nephew, there is no food in the land because of the famine, so there is nothing that I can give you to take home," Nyang said with sadness in her voice.

As Awan was about to leave, Nyang told him to wash all her eggs before his departure. Awan agreed and entered the cage, brought out an egg, which he washed, and showed it to Nyang, and said, "Is that not clean?"

"It is clean, my nephew. Take it inside," Nyang said. Awan then took the egg into the house. But while inside he rolled the egg in the dust until it became dirty. He then brought it out, washed it again, and turned to Nyang.

"My aunt, is it not clean?"

"It is clean my nephew. Take it inside," Nyang replied.

After Awan had washed the egg nine times, he finally washed it for the tenth time and turned to Nyang.

"My aunt is this clean?" Awan asked as he was showing the egg to Nyang.

"It is clean, my nephew," Nyang said.

"My aunt, can you allow me to take an egg as a gift?" Awan asked.

"Why are you impatient? I told you to wash the egg because I know what I was going to do. You can take that one," Nyang told Awan.

"I am very pleased, my aunt," Awan said.

After he was given the egg, Awan hurriedly left for his home. Soon after that, Nyang entered her house and opened the cage. She was shocked to find that there was a problem with the eggs. That prompted her to check all of them, one by one. To her surprise Nyang discovered that they were all light, just empty shells. Nyang came out, wailing. She did not want to lose a moment, so she rushed to the river to get Awan before he could escape by canoe. By the time Nyang arrived at the river bank, Awan was already in the canoe and in the middle of the river. Nyang called loudly: "Fishermen rowing the boat, overturn the boat to drown Awan. He has destroyed my home."

The people rowing with Awan asked, "Adukuäu, what is Nyang saying?"

Awan twisted Nyang's words to: "Nyang is saying: 'people rowing the boat, paddle the boat faster to take my nephew across the river. The storm is approaching. Do not delay.'"

As a result of that, the fishermen doubled their efforts in rowing the canoe towards the other bank.

Since the boat people were doing the opposite of what Nyang was saying, Nyang became angry. But she continued, again and again shouting aloud, "People rowing the boat, overturn the boat to drown Awan. He has destroyed my home."

"Adukuäu," asked the people rowing the canoe, "What is Nyang saying?"

Awan reported the same words. Nyang was telling them to row fast to take him to the other bank before the storm.

In despair, Nyang finally plunged into the water, hoping to catch up with the boat people and Awan.

At that stage, the fishermen heard what Nyang was saying and overturned the canoe, sliding Awan overboard into the water. Nyang rushed in, caught up with Awan.

"Nyang caught up the floating weeds and wished she had caught up with Awan." When Nyang heard this, she let go of Awan and she caught up with the floating weed, Awan said again, "Nyang let go of Awan and caught up with the floating weed and wished he he caught up with Awan."

In the water, Awan briefly bullied Nyang, making her move to and fro between himself and floating swamp grass. Then Awan swam out of the river to the land from where he sprinted into the forest.

Nyang remained on shore, still fuming with anger over the damage Awan had done- having eaten her nine eggs in addition to the one that she had given him on the day he was leaving.

In the forest, Awan broke the egg, drank the yolk, and carried the shell. On his way he found two antelope bulls fighting; he dropped the shell under their legs.

The bulls crushed the shell with their hooves.

"What have you done?" Awan said and added: "You have broken my egg. The only egg for which I have destroyed the home of my maternal aunt. Can my egg end up here? Wheew *Riardiën-ci-riar-awën.*[1] Bring my egg immediately or I do will do the worst to the two of you."

Awan was given a huge lump of bushmeat, which he took and left. On the way he found a woman who had just given birth, drinking the soup made out of a cow's placenta. He took pity on her, so he gave her the bushmeat he was carrying home. After he had given it he added:

"If there is something coming after me, swooshing noisily putput/*puɔt puɔt* like a wind, it is not me. If it comes, whispering softly liire/*liirë* like cold, it is me," Awan said and left.

In the nearby forest, Awan went and transformed into a wind. And he came swooshing noisily in dust and took away the meat. And again, in a short space of time Awan came back, whispering softly and he asked:

"Where is my bushmeat?"

"It was taken by the wind," the relatives of the woman said.

"What?" Awan shouted, "My egg, for which I had senselessly destroyed the home of my maternal aunt in a worst ever disaster. For my egg I was given my bushmeat. Can it end up this way here?

Riardiën-cï-riaar-awën! Bring my bushmeat immediately or I will cause havoc here now," Awan threatened.

Awan was given a string of beads, made of *abek*[2] (ostrich eggshell). He took the beads and left. On the way he found a bride being taken to her husband. She was wearing *naai* (a string of fibres of the dom tree) on her neck instead of beads. Awan gave out the beads to the bride. After he had given it he added:

"If anything comes after me, swooshing noisily like a wind, it is not me. If it comes, whispering softly like cold, it is me," Awan said and left.

Awan went into the nearby grass, changed into wind and he returned, swooshing noisily and carried away the beads. After a while Awan returned whispering sofly and he asked:

"Where is my bead?"

"It is taken by the dusty wind," the relatives of bride said.

"What?" Awan shouted, "My egg, for which I had senselessly destroyed the home of my maternal aunt in a worst ever disaster. For my egg I was given beads. Can it end up this way here? *Riardiën-cï-riaar-awën*! Bring my beads immediately or I will cause havoc here now," Awan threatened.

Awan was given *rëët* (a razor blade), he took and it left.

31

Awan went and found girls in the forests, shaving their pubic hair with cowrie shells (*gaak de-acööm*). Awan gave the razor blade to the girls. After he had given it he added:

"If there is something coming after me, swooshing noisily like a wind, it is not me. If it comes, whispering softly breeze, it is me," he said and left.

In the nearby forest, Awan went and converted himself into a whirlwind, and he shot back like an arrow and took it in a cloud dust. Within a short time, he returned transformed as Awan of the flesh.

"Where is my blade?" Awan asked.

"It was taken by a whirlwind," the girls said.

"What?" Awan shouted, "My egg, for which I had senselessly destroyed the home of my maternal aunt in a worst ever disaster. For my egg I was given bushmeat. For my meat, I was given strings of beads. For my beads I was given a razor blade. Can it end up this way here? *Riardiën-cï-riaar-awën*! Bring my blade immediately or I will cause havoc here now," Awan threatened.

Awan was given an axe, which he took and left. Awan went and found men cutting trees with wooden shovels.[3] Awan gave the axe to the men and left. Soon after that he returned.

"Where is my axe?" he asked.

"The axe is broken," the men replied.

"What?" Awan shouted, "My egg, for which I had senselessly destroyed the home of my maternal aunt in a worst ever disaster. For my egg I was given an axe. Can it end up this way here? *Riardiën-cï-riaar-awën!* Bring my axe immediately or I will cause havoc here now," Awan threatened.

Awan was given a fishing spear, which he took and left. Awan went and found boys, who were fishing with pointed sticks, he gave the fishing spear to them and left. When Awan returned from hunting in the forest, he found the fishing spear had loosened from the shaft and dropped into water.

"Where is my fishing spear?" Awan asked.

"Your fishing spear has fallen into the water," the boys said.

"What?" Awan shouted, "My egg, for which I had senselessly destroyed the home of my maternal aunt in a worst ever disaster. For my egg I was given bushmeat. For my meat I was given strings of beads. For my beads I was given a razor blade. For my blade I was given an axe. For my axe I was given a fishing spear. Can it end up this way here? Riardiën-cï-riaar-awën! Bring my fishing spear immediately or I will cause havoc here now," Awan threatened.

Awan was given the fattest catfish out of all the fish but he rejected. "I want a fish which is alive," Awan demanded. Awan was given another big mudfish but rejected it. "I want a living fish," Awan demanded. The boys entered the water and caught a small Akonthok fish alive and they gave it to Awan. Awan accepted it. After receiving Akonthok, he left for a nearby pond which he found was dry, without a drop of water. Awan left the dry pond and went to another pond which was full of water and asked, "You pond, when will you dry up?"

"I will dry very soon," Pond replied.

"You are acursed pond, I will leave you," Awan said and went to another pond.

"You pond, when will you dry up?"

"I will not dry up until the next rain arrives," Pond said.

"You are my best friend, Pond," he said and then dropped Akonthok in the water, and he left for his home.

In the morning Awan returned to the pond and while he was standing on its edge, he called out: "Akonthok, Awan's fish, come out so that we go out to eat berries from the nearby bush."

Akonthok hurried out of the pond. Awan was very pleased that his fish had grown up very fast overnight to the size of his arm. Awan and Akonthok went to the forest. In the evening they returned, with Akonthok returning into the pond and Awan to his home. For a

long time, Awan had been coming every day to pick Akonthok to gather berries for their meals.

During that long time, Köör the Lion who was in a nearby thicket, was secretly and closely watching Awan as he was talking to Akonthok. One morning Köör went to the pond to lure Akonthok out of the water. He called Akonthok to come out and meet him. Akonthok heard the speaker whose voice he recognised as that of Köör although he had changed it-pretending to be Awan- for deception.

Akonthok refused to come out of the pond. Köör

called out several times, but Akonthok refused to leave the safety of the water. Köör left quickly before Awan could arrive.

Awan, a short while after Köör's departure from the pond, while standing on its edge, called out: "Akonthok, Awan's fish, come so we go picking sweet berries from the bush."

Akonthok emerged from the pond to meet Awan, who became glad to see Akonthok.

Awan and Akonthok went out together to the forest. In the evening they returned to the pond. Akonthok dived into the pond and Awan left for his home.

That afternoon Köör went and called Agaal the Stork for help.

"Agaal, my friend, I have a plan. I would like you to help me with that. I want you to lure- with your sweet voice- Akonthok out of of the pond," Köör said.

"What is that?" Agaal asked.

"It is Awan's fish in the pond," Köör replied.

On the following morning, before Awan's arrival, Köör and Agaal had went to the pond. Agaal cleared his throat and tuned his voice down as much as possible to resemble Awan's accent.

"Akonthok, Awan's fish, come out, so we go to eat berries in the forest," Agaal called as he was imitating Awan's voice.

Deceived, Akonthok immediately jumped out of the pond. But when he saw Köör and Agaal together, he was shocked and as he was trying to return into the pond, it was too late for him. Köör sprang into action and caught Akonthok and killing him, cut the fish to pieces and he hurriedly carried it to his home.

Shortly after Köör had gone, Awan arrived at the pond.

"Akonthok come out, so we go to eat sweet berries in the forest." There was no response, but dead silence from the pond. Awan called several times, but there was no sign of Akonthok.

"What has happened to my fish?" Awan asked himself. When he looked round the pond area, he saw some birds clustering over an object on the other side of the pond. Awan went there to see what was happening.

"What are you doing here friends?" Awan asked the birds.

"These are lies (koiyɔ̈ɔ̈i)," Adöl the Ibis answered.

"What lies?" Awan asked.

"We do not know," one of the birds told Awan.

"I will fight and kill all of you if you do not tell me what you are eating," Awan threatened the birds.

"If you ruffle my feathers, you will comb them until they become as beautiful as they always are?" Adöl enquired.

Awan began to draw signs on the ground with his hands, looking in the opposite direction until he abruptly captured Adöl, as the other birds walked away. Awan held Adöl and began to repeatedly slap him on the head.

"Leave me, I will tell you what has happened," Adöl pleaded.

"Tell me now quickly. What are you doing here?" Awan asked.

"We are feeding on fallen off pieces from your fish," Adöl replied.

"What has happened to my fish?" Awan asked.

"Köör killed your fish, cut it and carried it to his home," Adöl said.

When Awan heard that, he let Adöl loose and went straight to Köör's den. Awan found a blind old Köör grandMother, *Dan cïï thuët*, and *Dan thuët*,[4] in a leather apron hung up on a pole at the home. The rest of the pride were absent. They had gone for the dance and Akonthok was in the pot, being cooked.

Awan ran to a nearby pond, where he picked up Aguek, and asked him, "How do you cry, Aguek?"

"What do you mean? Do you not know that I am Aguek? I croak as all members of family Aguek do," he said.

Awan threw him away and told him, "You are not the type of Aguek I am looking for," he complained and left.

Awan went to another pond, where he picked up another Aguek.

"Show me how you croak," Awan asked him.

"I roar like like *Dan de Köör* (Lion's cub)," Aguek replied.

"Very good. Now you are my friend, the best type of Aguek," Awan said.

Awan carried Aguek to Köör's den and quietly sneaked in. Awan ate his fish out of the pot and killed the cub, which he put in the pot, poured water over it, and started the fire under it to boil.

After that Awan placed a piece of wood in a leather apron, which resembled a Lion's cub. He used that for concealing Aguek inside it. Awan then hung the load on a pole. After that he signalled Aguek to roar like a Lion's cub, which he did convincingly. When Köör's GrandMother (Lionness) heard that, she began to shake him and sang a lullaby for him.

Awan was tickled when he saw the old blind Köör grandMother doing that to Aguek who had been disguised.

It was midnight when Awan went to the dance ground that was swarming with happy dancers, who were singing and enjoying themselves with abundance in the moonlight atmosphere. Awan joined in, dancing and singing his song, 'The Bubbling Cub:'

Some Lions are dancing,
While their Cub is cooking,
Boiling and bubbling in the pot,
Guok Guok Guok.[5]

When a member of the Pride heard the Awan's song, he asked, "Adukuäu, what are you saying?"

Awan twisted the Bubbling Cub into another song, 'Dazzling cow,' and said he was singing the song that ran this way:

You Girls,
Who are going to the cattle camp,
Take with you the rope of my cow,
The Dazzling cow,
A famous cow to girls and boys,
And by everyone in the land.

"Adukuäu, your song is great. Continue singing it," Köör, who had questioned Awan, remarked.

After that Köör returned to the dance grounds.

Awan began to sing his Bubbling Cub refrain again.

Another Köör heard him, and asked Awan, "Adukuäu, what are you saying in your song?"

Awan again changed the Bubbling Cub to Dazzling cow.

Then Köör heard it and said, "You have sung a beautiful song and your singing was melodious."

During the dance, Awan had been singing the Bubbling Cub version when the Pride heard and tried to question what the lyrics were referring to, he kept on switching the song to Dazzling cow wording.

When the dance was over, the participants dispersed to their various places where they had come from. For their part, the Pride went to their dens, where they ate Akonthok. Following that, Köör told the Pride that their older Cub, who had been left at home refused to eat Akonthok.

"Eat your fish, my child. Why are you not eating the fish?" Köör wondered.

"I cannot eat my MIMI (a sound being murmured by the Cub) whose rings of the hand and abek [6] (string of beads) of the neck remained in the pot. The black eye Aguek is croaking," *Dan cï Dëu* (older Cub) babbled.

Köör did not understand what the older cub was saying.

"Do you want to eat with your grandMother?" Köör asked.

"I cannot," said the older Cub.

The older Cub kept murmuring, repeating to its parents what was incomprehensible to the rest of the Pride. They were puzzled and failed to understand what the Cub had been saying.

Thus, the Cub's Father (Köör) went to bring Seer, who could unravel what the Cub was saying. Köör first brought Gak, the Crow. Gak glided in a long circle and landed. "If the grains are roasted and scattered on the floor and I pick them up with my beak, I will be able to reveal what the Cub is saying," Gak said.

The roasted grains were scattered on the ground. Gak picked them up and the Cub was brought before him. After singing the hymn, Gak asked him, "What is the problem with you, Cub?"

"I cannot eat my MIMI whose rings of hands and beads of the neck remained in the pot. The black eye Aguek is croaking," the older Cub said.After a lengthy search for the meaning of what the Cub was saying, Gak flew away, an indirect admission of his failure to solve the mystery.

The Father brought the Chuoor, the Eagle. Chuoor said, "If you slaughter an Ox to feed all the Vultures, and I were to be *Bäny Bith*[6] nibble its heart alone, I would be able to reveal what the Cub is babbling about."

An ox was sacrificed after Chor (Vultures) had picked the flesh off the Ox's bones, the Cub was brought before him and Chuoor said, "What is the problem, Cub?"

"I cannot eat my MIMI whose rings of hands and

beads of neck remained in the pot. The black eye Aguek is croaking," older Cub said.

After a long deep divine searching in his head of what the Cub was talking about, Chuoor the Spearmaster without admitting that he had failed, flew away as he was being chased by other vultures.

"Who will solve this mystery? If anyone manages to reveal it to me, I will give that soothsayer ten cows," Köör promised.

There was a meeting, some members of the Pride said it is Ibis the Seer to reveal it. Others said it was Awet the Crane who would reveal it. The Father of Cub went and brought Awet.

Awet came with other cranes; among them was Duket the songster and Agamlong/*Agamlɔŋ* the interpreter. Without asking for anything Awet told the pride to bring the older Cub forward.

The Songster started up the hymn. The cranes sang the hymn in praise of Jok (Jɔk) the Divine Spirit, reaching the excellent and sonorous verse of it, Jok caught up Awet, trembling him up and down in divine hullabaloo and he then spoke through Agamlong.

"Kuluk ku..." Awet said in the divine language, which the pride could not understand.

"Köör, Awet is cracking the puzzle," Agamlong interpreted it loudly.

"Blessed be Awet, the spirit of my ancestors," Köör exclaimed.

"Balak ka...," Awet intoned.

"Köör Mother (Lioness), Awet is unravelling the mystery," Agamlong said.

"Good outcome, Jok (Spirit) of our ancestors," Köör roared.

When the pride failed to understand the mysterious language, Awet was requested to speak in ordinary language.

"Awet, speaks in Lion's language, your children (Lions) do not understand your divine language," Agamlong said.

"What are you saying, Cub?" Awet asked.

"I cannot eat my MIMI whose rings of hands and beads of the neck remained in the pot. The black eye Aguek is croaking," the older Cub said.

"Mother of Cub," Awet called.

"Yes," the Mother of Cub answered.

"Your Cub has been babbling 'MIMI' sound, hasn't it?" Awet asked.

"Exactly, MIMI is the sound my older Cub has been babbling along," the Mother of Cub answered.

"Well, listen carefully now," Awet began, "This is the meaning of the mystery, "MIMI," means I cannot eat my brother. This is so because you Köör had stolen

Akonthok, Awan's fish. When you were at the dance, Awan came home, ate his fish, killed your youngest Cub and put him in the pot, cooking him. Awan put a frog in the apron skin, who is croaking in it now. So, what you have eaten is not a fish but your own Cub. Therefore the older Cub is refusing to eat his brother. Awan went to the dance ground, too, and he informed you by singing his loaded song, Bubbling Cub but you did not understand the loaded song.

When the pride heard this, a frightening silence pre-vailed all over the place; everyone was looking at ev-eryone's eyes with sickness. There was a strong denial of eating of the Cub.

"I have not tasted my cub," Köör denied as she vomited severely.

The aunt of the dead Cub jumped into the hut, brought out the Aguek and threw it down and trampled it under her feet as she denied eating the Cub.

Everyone denied that they had eaten the Cub.

"Stop it," Awet ordered, "Köör, run and fetch an ox to be sacrificed on arrival."

Köör did as advised. Awet sacrificed the ox, after which he sprinkled all members of the pride with mixture of blood blended with cud. That act was a form of blessing. He ordered that the meat of the sac-rificed ox, being a taboo, should not be consumed, but instead had to be dragged to the forest and discarded for the beasts and birds in the wild to feed on.

After the rites had been performed, Köör the Father gave ten cows to Awet as a reward, but he refused them. He preferred to be given only a heifer, which he took and left for his home.

No sooner had Awet left then the pride set out to kill Awan. Some mud was built on one of Köör's knee joints and filled up with churned milk. And the pride sent a messenger to tell Awan that one of his relatives had a swollen knee joint and that needed to be operated so the pus could come out. Awan accepted the request and told the messenger to go ahead and that he was going

When Awan was going to the den, he tied many tufts of elephant grass across the footpath. Arriving at the den, Awan found the sick Köör lying supine on the floor and surrounded by family members. Awan squatted beside him, and he touched the swollen knee joint slightly. "It is in a bad shape and to be rectified as soon as possible," Awan declared. He then turned around and saw the pride had surrounded him, and were looking at him menancingly.

"Why do you circle around me like this, and how shall I dodge the spurting pus, you open one side?"

The pride opened one side.

Awan pierced the swelling and suddenly a white churned milk poured down, not pus, and Awan ran away. One of the Lions threw a spear at Awan, but he missed him. All other Lions were now chasing Awan; however, they were stumbling, and falling down on the path because of the tied grass-tufts, and Awan was jumping the tied grass-tufts, escaping them into the thicket.

"Awan survived again," cried Köör of the child.

The Pride made another plan to kill Awan; they gave one of their daughters to Awan as a wife. The marriage was a trick to get Awan. Awan agreed and married Köör's daughter. One day, the wife of Awan went to her parents' home. Her parents asked her: "Where do you sleep with Awan?"

"We sleep in the hut," the girl told her parent.

The Pride said, "We shall burn your house tonight, so you sleep with your hands out, so we shall catch your hands and pull you out of fire."

By the time, Awan's wife was talking to her parents, he was hiding and snooping in the farm. And because of that Awan was able to know all that was being said. When his wife returned home, Awan said to her, "If you are the wife, the one I obtained by means of my Father's herds of cattle, give me these ivory bangles you are wearing on your arms."

The wife gave the bracelet to Awan.

That night the Lions came and burned Awan's house. Awan gave out his hands, the pride saw the ivory bangles on the hands, they thought it was their daughter; they pulled Awan out from fire and threw him behind them. In the darkness Awan ran to the bush. When Köör's daughter was crying in the fire, the pride refused to pull her out because they said it was Awan deceiving them again. Later the pride found it was their daughter who had been burned inside the house.

"Awan has escaped death again," the pride said.

After that escape, the Lions had been hunting for Awan. One day by chance they got to his stable. It was a stable built without door. Awan built it without doors, and he dug a long hole in the middle that has an opening in the forest as a door. At night, the pride came and called, "Awan, where are you?"

"Yes, but who are you?"

"It is us," said the pride.

"What do you want from my stable at night?" Awan asked.

"Killer, come out," the pride shouted.

"No, I am not coming out," Awan said.

"Then we will set your stable on fire," the pride said.

The pride immediately set the stable on fire. Awan escaped through the tunnel within the the stable that led into the nearby forest.

While the stable was on fire, the pumpkins in the stable exploded. Köör began to celebrate outside on learning what was happening. "Awan that is what you deserve," he boasted. After the stable had been burned to ashes, the pride left for their home.

As the pride was leaving, they saw Awan moving through the grass as he was on his way home. The pride, who could not believe their eyes, were shocked and disappointed by the trick Awan had played with them. They did not want to lose time and set out to chase the cunning Awan, but it was all in vain because he managed to escape.

Glossary

[1]*Riardiën-cï-riar-awën* this is a type of exclamation expressed by someone expressing displeasure with someone else over an issue on which the two disagree; it is a kind making disagreement being explicitly declared. At another level, the remark is usually expressed in sombre tone, and can be a self-congratulory expression of someone who has achieved what could be considered as a feat. These include someone throwing a weapon at an object and the missile directly hits the target. The person throwing the missile then jumbs up shouting words of self praise. Okot p'Bitek, the Ugandan writers calls this kind of ululation "*moch*," which the Dinka version is *miöc / muɔc*. In other dialects of the Dinka, it is called *waar*, in other dialects it is *guak*.

[2] *Dan cïï thuët*: in Dinka this means a cub that was too old to depend on Mother's milk, while *dan thuët* is a cub that was still a suckling. *Dan* is a genitive case of *dau*, which a young (usually female) animal, usually that of a domestic animal such as a cow, goat, sheep.

Lions, *Köör* pl *kɔɔr* (here rendered as a Pride).

[3] Wooden shovels: in the olden days, a long, sharpened log was made to be used as a hoe for ploughing and digging holes. In Dinka it is called *agoot* (*agɔɔt*)

[4] Pride: a group of Lions. Lion in Dinka is *köör* as single but plural is *kɔ̈ɔ̈r*. To avoid confusion between single and plural, Pride is used instead of *kɔ̈ɔ̈r*.

[5] Guok Guok Guok: This is onomatopoeia, as defined by a dictionary as "a word that phonetically imitates, resembles, or suggests the sound that it describes." In Dinka, the words are written *Guɔk Guɔk Guɔk*.

[6] *Abek*: A string of beads made from the shell of an ostrich egg.

[7] *Dan cï Dëu*: In Dinka this means a calf that is old enough to have given up feeding from the Mother cow.

[8] *Dan thuët*: Dinka expression meaning; calf that is still very young, a suckling.

[9] *Bäny Bith*: literally this means 'Spear Master,' someone claiming to have spiritual powers.

The Hyena and the Sheep

Once upon a time Amaal the Sheep, was walking in the forest. Angu, the Hyena, saw him. He began to crawl in the grass towards Amaal. When Amaal noticed an unidentified object moving in the grass in his direction, he stopped to listen and scan the grassy area.

"One should not flee from an unidentified object even if that happens to be a living creature," Amaal said to himself as he wanted to dismiss his fears. He carefully surveyed the area around him but saw nothing to worry about, so he continued walking along the path.

Angu suddenly appeared behind Amaal, and instantly seized Amaal. Taken off guard, Amaal sent out a loud scream, calling out for help. Angu laughed and told Amaal no matter how loud he cried, nothing would save him because he was going to kill him soon.

"I know this is my end, but you will do nothing to kill my spirit that is crying," Amaal told Angu.

"You are at my mercy, but I will allow you to escape. If you abuse the mercy of Jok, the Creator, he will not blame me for killing you and feeding on your carcass," Angu said.

"Give me that chance and I will try my luck," Amaal pleaded.

"Promise me three conditions and I will spare your life," Angu declared.

"But what will happen if I keep those three conditions that are false, will you not harm me after that?" Amaal wanted to know.

"I swear by Chok[1] that I will not harm you," Angu assured Amaal.

"You may be right, but later when I tell members of my species that Angui had captured me but released me without doing any harm to me, none of them will believe me," Amaal replied

"You are right in that," Angu said.

"The second point is that you are not hungry

because you have had enough food today and do not need any more food now," Amaal added.

"In the second point you are right again, and I agree with you," Angu said.

"The third point is that you have fed on the carcasses of several domestic and wild animals," Amaal said.

"Again, I agree with you on this third point," Angu said.

With those answers from Amaal, Angu accepted defeat and allowed Amaal to go, saying, "Amaal, you can now go. With your wisdom you have escaped death that was unavoidable. Go and tell all the beasts in the land and in the air, whether living with human beings or free in the wild, that cows, straying into my path in the forest, the only thing that will save them from certain death is their wits," Angu said and left.

Glossary

[1] Chok (cɔk): is Dinka word for hunger or famine.

An Incredible Truth

O nce upon a time a successful hunter known as Ayieep[1] lived in a village.

One day while he was walking in the forest, Ayieep stumbled on Awan the Fox, who had fallen into a trap. Ayieep ran home and he shouted the loudest alarm: "Elephant, Elephant is trapped in hole." About 40 men went out with spears and they found it was not an Elephant but Awan. When the men returned, some of them were angry, while others were laughing.

One day, Ayieep moved from the village to the cattle camp. When the men inquired about his health and and the condition of their kin and kith in the village, Ayieep told the famous Singer: "Your Mother had stolen and slaughtered a goat."

When the Singer went to the village, he discovered that Ayieep had told a lie.

When Ayieep returned to the village he was asked about the situation in the cattle camp. He said the cattle had been been raided by rustlers and that many young men been had killed while fighting the raiders.

On hearing that story the village people went into shock. The village people rushed to the cattle camp to see what had happened and what they could do. On arrival at the camp, they found that Ayieep had told a lie.

Throughout the land Ayieep became notorious for the lies he told.

The Singer came to dislike Ayieep and disbelieved and rejected everything he said. The Singer told everyone that he would remain in his place and would not run for safety if Ayieep were to sound an alarm about an imminent attack by a band of enemies.

One afternoon, Ayieep was collecting dry stalks in his farm. Suddenly the Singer, who Ayieep had one time deceived (that his Mother had stolen a goat), came running, being chased by some people who had caught him seducing a woman.

"They want to kill me. What will I do?" the Singer asked.

"You hide within in these stalks," Ayieep advised him.

The Singer hid himself in the tall, leafy grain stalks. Ayieep covered him up with more stalks.

When the men chasing him arrived, they asked about the whereabouts of the Singer.

"Where is the man who came running?" one of his pursuers asked.

"He is hiding behind these stalks," Ayieep showed the purusers the Singer's location.

"We cannot believe this because Ayieep is a chronic liar," one of the men objected.

"The man is not hiding behind these stalks. Let us leave. He is just delaying us with his lies," another man complained.

All the men who were pursuing the Singer agreed that Ayieep was an inveterate liar. As a result of that they decided to give up the search for the Singer, and they left the scene.

After the men had gone, the Singer emerged out of the stalks and asked Ayieep,

"Why did you tell those people about where I was?"

"I told them that you were hiding from them there in the stalks," Ayieep said.

"What if they had killed me?" the Singer wondered.

"Should they have killed you, it would have been a testimony that I speak nothing but the truth," Ayieep boasted.

"The divinities of your ancestors have saved me, but despite that you remain the ultimate liar that has ever lived," the Singer declared.

"Yes, I will be a liar to others, but you can bear witness that I told the truth about where you were hiding although your enemies never believed me," Ayieep contended.

Glossary

[1]Ayieep (*ayiëëp*): A Dinka word for hunter. This is derived from *yäp* or hunting.

Jok's Child, the Fox, and the Vulture

O nce upon a time, Menh e Jok,[1] the Child of the Creator and Awan went to steal cattle from humans. As they were preparing for the raid, Awan told Menh e Jok that they should carry some food to eat on the way.

Awan proposed that each of them take a large calabash containing food and a gourd full of water. Their food and water were prepared and put in big calabashes and gourds. When they were about to leave, Menh e Jok said he did not want the big calabash and gourd, and that he instead wanted to carry a little calabash and gourd, arguing that: "Offspring from honourable families[2] as we are, should not demean themselves to carry large food and too much water while on a mission." So, the food and water of Menh e Jok were changed from the big calabash and gourd to the small calabash and gourd. However, Awan continued to carry his big calabash and gourd arguing that, "He was carrying the big calabash and gourd not because of gluttony but because the journey was long."

The following morning, the two set off for the raid. They walked the whole morning. At about midday when the heat of the sun became unbearable, they decided to rest under the shadow of a large tree. While resting they began to eat food and drink water. When the weather turned cool in the afternoon the two resumed their journey. By midnight, they stopped to sleep.

After they had walked for many days in the forest, Awan ran out of food and water but Menh e Jok had been eating his food out of the calabash, and the food kept filling the calabash. Whenever he drank his water in the little gourd, the water kept filling the gourd.

After Awan had finished his food and water, he had to depend on Menh e Jok's food and water. And they contiuued looking for herds of cattle to steal.

One afternoon, Menh e Jok became angry, and consequently destroyed his calabash of food and gourd

FOLKTALES FROM SOUTH SUDAN

of water, accusing them of their failure to find the the cattle they were looking for.

"Why have you done this, Menh e Jok, my brother? Will we not die of hunger and thirsty?" Awan wondered.

"Who told you that offspring from honourable families, as we are, can die of hunger or thirst? Let us proceed," Menh e Jok urged Awan.

The pair resumed their search that morning. On the way they found a pond full of water, whose water had been muddied by birds which had been fishing there.

"Can we drink this water, Menh e Jok, my brother?" Awan asked.

"Never! Offspring from honourable families, as we are, should not demean themselves to drink such dirty water as this," Menh e Jok asserted.

After that they resumed their search for cattle. After a long walk that afternoon, Awan became thirsty, and he told Menh e Jok he was not able to walk any further. Menh e Jok stopped and began to think of what they should do to find water. He told Awan that they should look for *awaar*, a type of grass whose tubber-like roots contains water.

Awan pulled up the tuft of grass and cleanest water, but the grass was very difficult to be uprooted from its base. Awan applied all his strength and he wrenched out the grass from its base. Inspite of all that effort Awan failed. For his part, Menh e Jok succeeded in pulling out the grass with its tubber swollen with tasty and cool water to drink.

To celebrate the lucky strike, and with one hand, he just pulled up the tuft of grass and cleanest water flowed out from its root. Awan poured the water over his head and then over his body before he could drink.

"My body should drink first before I drink through my mouth," Awan said.

"For me, I do not drink often. I can even walk for ten days without drinking any water," Menh e Jok claimed.

"Situations can force proud people to do things such as drinking dirty water if they are about to die of thirst," Awan explained.

After they had taken enough water, they resumed their search for cattle through the forest. Not long afterward, they found a carcass of Thiang,[3] the Roan Antelope, which had been partially eaten by birds.

"Can we pick the remnants of the flesh from the bones of this animal?" Awan asked Menh e Jok.

"Never! Offspring from honourable families, as we are, should not demean themselves to eat such things as this rotten meat," Menh e Jok protested.

"Why do you whatever I say should be done since

we started this mission, Menh e Jok?" Awan said, adding, "Do you think you are wiser than I am? I can stop from here and go back home?"

"Awan, my brother," Menh e Jok answered calmly, adding, "I have no bad intention. I refuse your ideas because they can tarnish the reputation of our honourable families. No harm can befall us, whether it is hunger, thirst or danger from wild animal and human beings."

After walking for some space of time, Awan was very hungry, and he could not walk any longer. Menh e Jok stopped and thought deeply about what to do to save Awan. He looked round, and he suddenly saw Menh e Jok and Thiang standing at some distance.

"Awan, my brother," called Menh e Jok, "Jump onto that anthill, and beckon Thiang among those standing there so that it come and fall down before us and skin itself and roast, so we eat it."

Awan climbed the anthill, and he beckoned to Thiang, but it stood still where they were standing. Awan failed. Menh e Jok splendidly climbed the anthill, and he beckoned the antelope, one antelope suddenly started running and bending on one side in a curving line until falling down before them, skinning itself and burning itself and they just started eating it. After they had eaten, they moved, walked for a short

time when Menh e Jok saw cattle grazing at a distance.

"Awan, my brother, what have you seen?" Menh e Jok asked.

"Nothing?" Awan asked again.

"Cattle," Menh e Jok replied.

Awan did not see them, to see properly, Awan covered his face with one hand to protect his eyes from the sun ray but still could not see the cattle. They had to walk again for another space of time before Awan could clearly see the cows.

They came over the grassland where the cattle were grazing. Menh e Jok and Awan selected for themselves the two most beautiful cows from the herd. With ropes they fastened the cattle and tied them to trees. In the shade of the tree, Menh e Jok lay down supine, and he told Awan to pluck his beard. As Awan was plucking Menh e Jok's beard, he saw the cattle owners approaching from far.

"Menh e Jok, my brother the cattle owners are coming, let us leave," Awan said.

"Just my mouth," Menh e Jok said.

Awan continued, while his eyes were on the enemies who were approaching and menancing.

"Menh e Jok, my brother," Awan said, shaking with fear, "The cattle owners have caught up with us. We should hurry away with the cattle."

"Remove my beard," Menh e Jok said.

Awan saw the men approaching.

"Menh e Jok, my brother," said Awan, "The cattle owners have arrived and will capture us."

Awan stopped removing the beard and attempted to run but the child of Jok held him down so that he could not run.

"*Akaacpiny-kuja-nhial-e-tung*!" Menh e Jok chanted his personality ox.

"Hold the rope tied to your cow, Awan, my brother and then catch my cow's tail," Menh e Jok said.

Awan caught them and Menh e Jok penetrated his head into earth; the earth opened up. Menh e Jok and

Awan disappeared. As they were travelling in the bowel of the earth, Menh e Jok began to blame Awan for what he said was a mistake, which he almost committed.

"Awan, my brother, why did you want to run in the bush? They would have captured and killed you. How disgraceful it would have been to our noble families if one of their respected sons had been killed in a cattle theft? And all types of theft are for people from lower classes. For us, we are stealing for fun, not for gain since we lack nothing," Menh e Jok stated.

"I was afraid," Awan confessed.

"How? Awan my brother," Menh e Jok wondered, "If you are a party to what I do no evil can befall you whether it is hunger or thirst, whether it is an enemy with a spear or with teeth," he said.

They were escaping down the bowel of the earth when there was no one seeing them until they reappeared in their home.

Some days passed and Awan went and called Chuoor[4] to go and steal cows with him. When they were preparing to leave for cattle raiding, Chuoor told Awan, they had to carry some food they would be eating on the way. Each of them was given a large calabash of food and gourd of water. Awan refused both and said, "Offspring from honourable families, such as we are, should not demean themselves to carry such large calabashes of food and gourd of water like the children of glutton." A little food was put in a small calabash and a small gourd was filled with water. Chuoor was carrying his load.

Early the following morning, Awan and Chuoor set out to search for cattle. They walked all morning until midday after which they stopped and sat in the shade of a tree. They had eaten their food and drank the water. Awan's calabash of food was not continuously filling as was the case with the calabash of Menh e Jok.

After Awan finished his food and water, he was eating and drinking from Chuoor. After they meandered in the forest for few days the food and water of Chuoor finished too.

After they had been wandering in the forest for long time, searching for cattle, they came over a pond full of water, which birds had fished and dusted.

"Awan, my brother, let us drink this water." Chuoor said.

"No. Offspring from honourable families, such as we are, should not demean themselves to drink such dirty water as this."

They left and moving for a while, the sun was very hot, the Chuoor became very thirsty; he could not walk any longer. Awan stopped and thought out what he should do to save his brother Chuoor, looking round, he saw tuft of grass (*awaar*). Awan told Chuoor to pull up the tuft of grass. Chuoor pulled out the grass and nothing came of it. Awan came and pulled up the tuft of grass too. There was no water flowing out of the grass hole. They were now dying of thirsty.

"Let us go back to pond of dirty water," Awan told the Chuoor. Awan and Chuoor returned and drank the dirty water that they earlier refused to drink. After drinking, they continued the search.

Moving and wandering through the forest looking for the cows, Awan and Chuoor found a carcass of Thiang, which the birds had partially eaten.

"Awan, my brother," said Chuoor, "Let us scratch the meat off the bones."

"No. Offspring from honourable families, such as we are, should not demean themselves to on such rotten meat as this."

They left the carcass. As they were walking and wandering in the forest searching for the cows, Chuoor became very hungry, and he could not walk any longer. Awan stopped and thought about what he should do to save his brother Chuoor, looking round, he saw some Thiang standing at some distance.

"Chuoor, my brother," Awan called, "Can you jump onto that anthill? And you signal Thiang among those standing there so it comes and falls down before us and skins and burns itself, so we eat it."

Chuoor climbed on anthill, and he beckoned the antelope. Thiang but it never came to them. Awan signalled Thiang never came to them, and they were very hungry. "Let us return to eat the rotten carcass," Awan said. They returned and ate the carcass they had first refused.

After eating they continued their search for cows, walking for a short space of time, they got the cattle and they selected for themselves, the best two among the cows. They tied the cows down on roots in shade under the tree. In the shade of the tree Awan lay down on his back and he told Chuoor to pick his beard. As he was picking his beard a certain spirit swooped on Chuoor's head.

"Awan, my bother," Chuoor called, "The cattle owners will come. Let us leave immediately."

"Just pick my beard," Awan said.

"Awan, my bother," Chuoor said, "The cattle owners may come. Let us leave immediately."

"Just pick my beard," Awan said.

Immediately, Chuoor saw the cattle owners were coming from far.

"Awan, the cattle owners are getting nearer," Chuor said.

"Pick my beards," Awan said.

"Awan, the cattle owners have arrived and are capturing us," Chuoor said.

"*Riardien-ci-riaar-awen!*" Awan chanted the metaphorical names of ox as he was getting up, held the rope of his cow and told the vulture to catch his cow's tail. Awan penetrated his head in the earth. The earth never opened itself up. Awan penetrated his head with more effort, but the earth never opened any hole. When Chuoor saw the cattle owners were about to capture them, Chuoor flew away, flapping its wings and sat on the treetop.

At last, Awan attempted to run but he was captured by the cattle owners. Awan was beaten until he fainted, and the men took their herd and left him.

After a very long time, Awan sneezed and opened his eyes, he saw Chuoor on the tree. Awan told Chuoor to bring him a thick stick so he would walk. Chuoor brought the stick, Awan turned it against Chuoor and beat him with it.

Glossary

[1]Vulture: *Chuoor* (*cuɔɔr*), plural *chor/cor*.

[2]Menh e Jok (*Mɛnh e Jɔk*): literarily this means child of God. Jok (Jɔk), means God, divinity, deity, creator, evil one, infectious or deadly disease. But in this context Jok means powerful one or creator.

[3]Offspring from honourable families: in plural this is; *mith ke adhueng* (*mïth ke adhuëŋ/adhëŋ*), while the singular is menh de adhueng / adheng (*mɛnh de adhuëŋ/ adhëŋ*).

Adheng / adhueng (*adhëŋ/adhuëŋ*), respected person, notable, nobleman. Dinka idiom "Menh de Adhëng" (*Mɛnh de adhëŋ/adhuɛŋ*) means a child from a noble or respected family.

[4]Thiang (*thiäŋ*): also Anglicised to Tiang, a kind of antelope.

The Fox, the Hyena, and the Hare

Once upon a time, Awan called Angu the Hyena to visit a friend with him. When they set out on the journey, each was carrying a bow and pouch of arrows. On the way they found the seashell [1] used for eating at the pond in the forest. Each of them picked for himself some of seashells and put them in their pouches. When they were about to reach the friend's home, Awan said they should throw away the seashell.

"It is not good to carry seashell to the home of friend, let us throw them away," Awan said.

All the seashells were thrown away. Walking for

a short space of time, they arrived the home of their friend. Their friend warmly welcomed them into his house. The friend told his wife to cook very good food for them.

When the friend's wife was cooking, Awan instructed her to cook the food and should bring it very hot in calabash and without a seashell for eating it. The wife cooked food and seasoned it with the butter of cow and took it to them as hot as fire as Awan instructed. When the food was brought, Awan sat upright on the papyrus mat and cleared his throat.

"Angu, can we shake our pouches?" Awan said.

Angu shook his quiver, and nothing fell out of it.

"Well, let me shake my pouch," Awan said.

Awan shook his pouch and a seashell fell down, so he bragged, "the quiver of mine sounded something jiling/jilinë while the quiver of the weakling sounds nothing but pap/päp." It appeared now that Awan had played a trick on the Angu at the time, they were throwing away seashells in the forest, because Awan had cunningly and secretly kept one and Angu had thrown away all his seashells.

"Angu, you run and go back to the place where we threw away our seashell to bring your seashell," Awan said.

Angu left immediately, running back to the forest to

bring his spoon. After Angu had left, Awan carefully removed the crust on the top of the food and he put it aside and he ate the whole food.

After that the Awan dropped rubbish in the calabash and put back a dry layer of food on his dung and urinating on it, he made his urine the butter to season the food. When Angu returned, the Awan told him that he had already eaten and so it was his portion of the food that was in the calabash.

When the Angu was eating the food, it was inedible, he asked the Awan why the food was tasting bad like that. The Awan replied he had no idea why the food tasted like that. And the Angu was very hungry he had to eat it in spite of its unfitness to eat.

In the evening the friend took them to sleep in one house with the goats. At midnight, the Awan woke up, killing a fat ram and he ate it. After eating the ram, he smeared Angu's mouth with blood while the Angu was deeply sleeping, and the blood dried on its mouth. In the morning the friend found one of his rams missing. When the Awan and Angu were checked, dried blood was found in the mouth of Angu. Angu was thoroughly beaten and fined to pay three goats.

The space of time passed, Awan went again and called Biol[2], as a companion to visit another friend's home. When they were travelling through a forest, they came over the pond full of spoons. Each picked some seashells for himself and put them in his pouch of arrows. They walked past some trees, Awan stopped, and he said,

"Biol, the giants like us cannot carry seashells, let us throw them away."

Awan and Biol threw away the seashells. Shortly they were in the friend's house, who warmly welcomed them, called his wife and he told her to cook for his friends the sweetest and most delicious food.

When the wife was leaving to go to prepare the food, Awan also added his own instruction, "And after you cook our food, you bring it when it is steaming hot without spoons to be used for eating."

The woman cooked and brought the food as hot as fire in a calabash without seashells as Awan had said. After the wife placed the food down, Awan sat up right in papyrus mat and cleared his throat to speak;

"Biol, can we shake what our pouches contain," Awan said.

Biol shook his pouch's stomach down and nothing fell out of it.

"Let me shake the contents down of my pouch," said the Awan.

Awan shook his quiver and a spoon fell down from it. "My pouch jiggled while the pouch of the weakling remained silent," Awan boasted as he picked up his spoon.

It appeared now that the Awan had played a trick on Biol at the time they were throwing away spoons in the forest, because Awan had cunningly and secretly kept one shell and Biol had honestly or had foolishly thrown away his spoons.

"Wife of our friend," Biol called, "Bring me a spoon."

"No, Biol, do not bother our friend's wife. You go and fetch the shells from the place where we had discarded them," Awan said.

Immediately Biol came out of the house, walked to the left side of the house, removed out one of his eyes, and secretly hid it in the low frame of the roof of the house in the grass. And Biol ran to bring his spoon in the forest.

After Biol had left, Awan sat happily and comfortably with his two legs, encircling the calabash. When he started eating the food, there a was voice, "Awan, why do you want to eat the food while Biol is not around." Awan panicked and his ears were curled up, scared, and ashamed. Awan stood up and looked around, but he did not see anybody because it was Biol's eye that was speaking.

When there was no one, Awan sat down again and tried to eat. "Awan, why do you want to eat the food while Biol is not around," the voice warned again.

Awan looked around and he did not see anyone,

but he only saw the lizard on roof, he said to himself it might be this Ariik the Lizard who was telling lies, he took a stick and killed the Ariik. And he sat down, and he tried started eating the food. The voice cried for the third time.

"Awan, why do you want to eat the food when Biol is not around." Awan came out of the house, he moved around the house, there was no one there. He returned into the house, he picked his spoon and he tried to eat.

"Awan, why do you want to eat the food when Biol is around," said the eye of Biol. Awan got up and said, "Who is this talking?"

From there Biol came back with his spoon. Biol's eye had kept disrupting Awan from eating the food until Biol arrived.

Biol took his eye where he left it and put it back into its place then he entered the house. As they were eating, Awan confessed to Biol that when he was spreading over the food, there was a voice calling and coming from nowhere, asking why he was eating the food when Biol was not around.

"And why did you spread the food when I was not around?" Biol asked.

"I was spreading it, so it gets cold," Awan said.

"Why did you do that when you were the one who

told the wife of our friend to bring it when it is hot?" Biol asked.

Listened to this, the Awan then shamefully kept silent, and they ate their food. Here the Biol became the first person who had cunningly beaten Awan for the first time.

When the night fell, they were taken to sleep in one house with goats. At midnight Awan woke and tried to kill the goat. Biol also woke and shouted, "Awan, what are you doing among the goats?"

With shame the Awan stopped and fell back and slept. Sleeping for a short space of time the Awan woke up and he wanted to kill the goat. Biol also woke and stopped Awan from killing the goat. Throughout the night the Awan had unsuccessfully been trying many times to kill the goat, but Biol had also been stopping him until daybreak.

In the morning, Awan was very angry because all his plans had shamefully been failed by Biol. Awan told their friend that they wanted to leave. Their friend gave them two pots of paste of groundnuts. Awan said he would carry his paste to his children at home, but Biol started eating his paste. After Biol finished eating his paste, they left for their village, Awan was carrying his pot of paste on his head.

When they had walked for a while in the forest, Biol

went and sat under the tree, saying he was tired, and resting and he told the Awan he would catch up with him on the way. Awan said okay, he left him and continued walking ahead.

After Awan had gone, Biol ran in the forest, bypassed Awan, went ahead of him, and transformed himself into fancy ebony stick and laid itself across the path.

Awan came over and he saw a nice stick on the way, he picked it and closely looked at it and throwing it away, saying, "Is this not Biol who has camouflaged himself like this?" And Awan continued walking.

Biol ran again in the forest, bypassed Awan and changed himself into a nice spear and lay itself across the path. Awan came over, saw it, picked it up, then looked at it closely and threw it into the grass, saying, "Is this not Biol who changed himself?" And Awan continued walking.

Finally, Biol ran in the forest, bypassed Awan, came up to the edge of Awan's farm, and changing himself haunch and lay itself on the edge of the farm to draw the red ants.

When Awan came and saw it, he was angry, he picked it up, shaking the red ants off it and he said; "What has my wife done bad like this?" She has let herself down here. I will beat her thoroughly." And

Awan put the haunch on the pot of the paste of the groundnut and he walked home. His wife saw him, rushed to welcome him, but he refused to greet her because he was angry.

"Do you have your thing?" Awan asked.

"Which thing are you asking?" the wife asked.

"Your haunch."

"Awan, have you lost your mind? Where do you think it has gone?" the wife asked while jeering at Awan.

Awan bursted into laughter, "I thought yours has fallen down because I found another one at the edge of the farm. Anyway, I have two haunches."

Awan gave the pot of paste to his wife. The wife placed it inside the house. The sun was setting.

At night Biol changed itself back and ate the paste and remained in the pot.

In the morning, Awan told his wife, "There is a paste in the pot, you bring it out and give half to the children and keep half for me."

The wife brought out the pot from the shelf, opening it Biol got out of the pot, ran, and skipped into the bush.

Awan threw the spear at Biol, but it missed him

The pot was empty. Awan was very angry with Biol.

In the following night, Biol returned, and he stole himself into Awan's stomach through Awan's backside while Awan was sleeping. When Awan awoke in the morning, he found Biol inside himself. Biol then peeped his out from Awan's backside.

Awan begged Biol to come out from his backside, but Biol refused. Biol, in jest, pinched Awan's bottom with his teeth and fingers. Biol was playing, pushing its nose in and out of the bottom

Using the sign language, so Biol could not hear what he was saying, Awan told his wife to put a fishing spear on the fire. After the fishing spear burned and became red hot, Awan told his wife to pierce the nose of Biol with it. When the wife tried to pierce Biol's snout, Biol saw the fishing spear and he quickly pulled back his nose inside and the fishing spear burned Awan's backside. Awan jumped in pain, crying to his wife, "Stop it, you are burning me."

When Biol heard Awan crying, he just chuckled inside. Awan and his wife tried to burn the nose of Biol, but ended up burning Awan's bottom several times.

It was impossible to harm Biol inside now. Awan went and tied grasses like human beings, he put spears in his hands, and he put the feather of the ostrich on their heads and put an empty gourd to the wind so that the wind hooted the gourd like a horn, and he said, "Biol now the human beings have surrounded us with spears, they want to kill us. Look at them, if you do not run, you will be killed."

When Biol peeped out, he saw the bundles of grass were standing exactly like human beings, Biol was frightened and afraid and he got out of Awan's backside. When Awan turned around and threw a spear at Biol, he missed him because he was already far away after he came out, running.

Glossary

[1]Thiet (*thiët*): seashells, singular: *thial*. Throughout the story "spoon" and "spoons" are used to refer to thial.

[2]Biol (*Biɔl*) is Hare. *Biɔl* in one of the Dinka dialects means something else- a rude word as it refers to part of a female genital. Here it means hare.

[3]Eyes/Nyin Biɔl: is a Dinka proverb for a spying/ acting on behalf of someone who is absent.

Angu, Awan and the Vulture

Once upon a time, Awan, Awan, and Chuoor the Vulture had their own cow. The cow gave birth to a calf and the calf died soon afterward. As a result, there was no calf to bring down the milk from the cow's udder. The Awan told the Angu and Chuoor he would be a new calf since he is a smallest among them, and Angu the Hyena would be the one to milk the cow. Both Awan and Chuoor agreed upon what Awan had said.

After Awan was then accepted as the new calf, he told again the Angu and Chuoor, he said, "If I am suckling out the milk from the cow, you shall not remove me from the udder, until I twist my tail, and if I forget to twist my tail, and the foam falls three times from my mouth, then you remove me, the milk is ready in the udder."

When it was a time for milking the cow, Angu released Awan to the cow and waited for him to twist his tail. Awan, instead of twisting his tail when the milk was ready, suckled out the whole milk from the udder. After he had finished the milk and was satisfied, he twisted his tail. Angu removed him, and he had to milk a very little milk. After Awan had suckled out the whole milk, he shared again the little milk with Angu and Chuoor. Through cheating his friend, Awan became fatter and stronger while Chuoor grew thinner and weaker.

One day the sister of Angu, who was married to man, came and she found her Angu very weak.

"Why are you thin, and miserable like this, Angu, do not you eat?" the sister of Angu asked.

"I do eat," Angu replied.

"Then, what is the problem?" the sister asked.

""There is nothing wrong with me , it is only that the calf of our cow has died ," Angu explained, "And Awan has made himself the new calf , who suckle the milk from the udder and I am the one who milked the cow. Awan also instructed me if he is suckling out the milk I should wait for him until he twists his tail before he would disrupt and remove him from the udder."

"Angu?" said his sister angrily, "You a grown up and you still you do not know tricks?"

In the morning, the sister of Awan took a big gourd and she released Awan to bring down the milk. And before Awan could twist his tail as usual, she suddenly and violently pulled him out from the udder, until the milk poured out of his mouth, and she tied him on the peg.

"What is this milk, you will break my heart?" Awan said, looking at Angu's sister with a black face, "I can stop stimulating this cow and I see how you will milk her. Without me stimulating the cow, you cannot milk her. It is not good to pull someone with force like that as if there is a problem."

"Stop talking!" Angu's sister shouted, "Which calf has ever talked like human?"

The cow was milked, and the milk filled the gourd to the brim. Awan, Angu and Chuoor sat, drank the milk until they were satisfied for the first time since Awan became the calf. For half a month, when Angu's sister had been milking the cow, Angu and Chuoor grew fat quickly.

When the Angu's sister was leaving, she instructed Angu to milk the cow in his style. Awan became angry.

One day, Awan went to tend the cow for the morning grazing. In the forest Awan smeared mud over the cow, changing it from white to black. And then Awan vigorously chased the cow back to the cattle camp. When Awan reached the camp's outskirts, he began to call.

"Angu take the spear, Thiang is entering the cattle camp."

Angu quickly took the spear and hit Thiang, killing it instantly.

"What have you done now?" Awan asked. "Why are you killing our cow?"

"But you called and told me it was Thiang," Angu complained.

"No! You should take ashes to groom the cow because of the flies," Awan stated.

"Why did you smear the cow with the mud?" Angu protested.

"It was to prevent flies from biting the cow," Awan explained.

Awan pretended he was very angry about what Angu had done. He said, "Nothing can be done since the cow is dead. I will skin the cow myself. Angu take the ayoth (basket) to bring water from the pond and you Chuoor, go up and bring fire from the sun."

Angu left for the pond to fetch the water.

Chuoor flew at the Sun to bring the fire.

After Angu and Chuoor left for their respective tasks. Awan started skinning the cow, cutting it into pieces. Then he carried the whole cow into his house to hide it. After that Awan dug a hole and put the head of cow in it and he left the horns up above the ground and he sat down under the nearby tree.

At the pond, Angu was drawing the water by basket. He put it on his head and returned. The water was leaking out from the basket before he reached home, because the basket was made of palm tree leaves. Angu had been fetching the water the whole day and the water had been leaking on the way, before he reached home. The leaking of the water had delayed Angu to return home until the sun was almost setting.

On the other hand, Chuoor flew to the sun. At the sun, it was difficult to take fire. When Chuoor tried to take fire, he flinched. The sun was hot, and several attempts to take the fire, made the sun burn Chuoor's hair. Chuoor had been trying to take the fire from the sun but it had been very difficult to take it because of the heat. When Chuoor saw that the sun was setting, he left the fire, but his hair was horribly burnt by the heat from the sun, making his head red and bald.

In the evening when Awan saw Chuoor and Angu were returning, he started running and calling, "Chuoor, Angu, Earth is swallowing our cow." Angu and Chuoor started running at once. The three arrived where Earth is swallowing the cow. They all caught the horns, holding them tightly and they pulled up the cow, falling backward, bumping their backsides on the ground, pulling out only the head.

"*Riardiën-ci-riaar-awen*! The Earth has swallowed the cow," Awan said, "My friends and my brothers, Earth has swallowed our cow, can you not give me this head as my share?" Awan begged.

"It will be done. Awan should take it," Angu said.

"What about us?" Chuoor angrily complained.

"But Angu what about you and me?" Chuoor angrily complained.

"You can have the head. What is the problem?" Awan told Chuoor.

"I have no problem. But the cow belonged to us. We should have shared the head, but Angu gave it to you. And we can share the head but since Angu gave it, you take it," Chuoor said.

That evening Angu's Sister heard what had happened it, so she came.

"Where is the cow?" Sister asked.

"I killed her by mistake and Awan sent me to bring water with a bucket and he sent Chuoor to bring fire from the sun. But when we returned, we found Earth had already swallowed the cow. We only pulled out the head out of the ground and Awan took it," Angu explained.

"Angu," his sister said, "You are mature enough to understand the world, but you can still be tricked to believe lies. Let us go to see Awan. Where is Chuoor?"

"Chuoor is here," Angu said.

"Call him," she said.

The Angu's sister was leading the way, Angu and Chuoor were following quietly. They arrived at Awan's home. They found a great feast in the house. There were many animals in Awan's house who were feeding off the cow. There was Menh e Jok, Kuach the Leopard, Nyang the Crocodile, Koor the Lion and Awet the Crane. It was only Akoon the Elephant, Biol the Hare and Liei the Cormorant who were absent because those three knew Awan and his cunning ways.

"Robber! Awan Robber!" shouted Angu's sister while rushing into the house to take the meat, "You divide the meat, or I will call my husband, the man and his brothers. How can Awan dare to cheat you, my brother?"

When Menh e Jok saw Awan was being threatened by Angu's sister with the power of human beings, Menh e Jok got angry.

"Can I do something my brother Awan," Menh e Jok asked.

"No, it is a minor problem. I will solve it," Awan said.

"Then tell that woman to stop."

"I pity her. She is only a woman," Awan said.

Finally, Awan divided the meat, giving Angu and other's their shares.

"Do not come to my home again," Awan warned Angu and Chuoor.

"Who will come to your place?"

Fox and Cormorant

O nce upon a time Awan and Liei [1] the Cormorant, the swampy water bird, met. Awan and Liei went together to the river bank. Arriving at the river's edge Liei told Awan, "Let me drink first." Awan agreed and allowed Liei to go and drink in the river. Liei went straight into the water and swam to the other bank.

"Were you deceiving me?" asked Awan

"Yes," answered Liei.

"Why did you deceive me?"

"You have been deceiving people all along."

Awan had known then that he could not get Liei, so he left. He went to the tree.

Glossary

[1]Liei (*liɛi*): cormorant.

Chapter 2

Majok Keeror the Famed Singer

O nce upon a time there were three brothers who used to go to dance far from their home. Akuur, their sister would want to go with them, but the brothers were seriously refusing her. In that dance the Lions had cleverly transformed themselves into men and danced there too. Every day after the brothers denied her going with them, Akuur would disobediently follow them.

And when Akuur was in the dance, she did not dance with any man, she refused to dance, and saying there was no man ever, who could sing a song sweet enough to make her dance. One dance day, a man who was called Majok Keeror came singing with his eyes tightly closed. The song ran:

Look at an ivory bracelet on my arm,
Look at the finest ivory of the handsome young man
Majok Keeror.

Look at the beads around my neck,
Look at the finest beads of an attractive young man
Majok Keeror.

Look at the beads of my waist,
Look at the finest beads of an attractive young man
Majok Keeror.

Look at the hairon my head,
Look at the finest hair of an attractive young man,
Majok Keeror.

Look at the rings on my legs,
Look at the finest rings of an attractive young man,
Majok Keeror.

My Mother is tired,
Of simmering the
Butter of ten herds of cattle.

My brother is tired
Of plaiting
The ropes for the herds of cattle.

My sister is tired
Of churning
The milk of the herds of cattle.

My Father is tired
Of slaughtering
Oxen to feed the guests.

When Akuur heard this song of Majok, she shouted, "Majok Keeror is the only man who has ever sung the most melodious song that I enjoyed very much indeed on this ground."

Opening his eyes, Majok saw Akuur already standing in front of him, crying the ululation of joy louder and louder, and swinging her neck backward and forward like the eagle. Majok danced alone with Akuur by singing many songs until the dance was over. At the end of the dance Majok had eloped with Akuur.

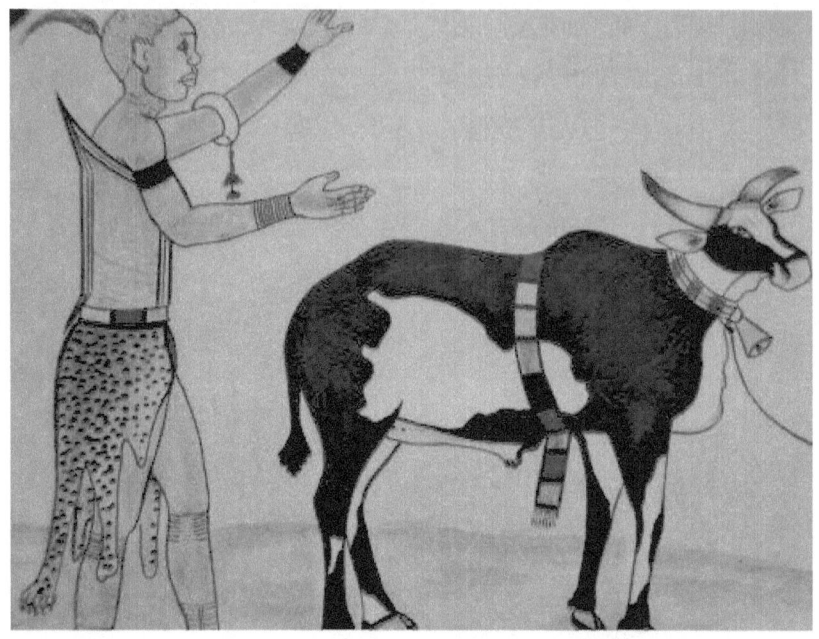

When arriving at home, Akuur was shocked when she found the first wife of Majok without fingers and toes. Her fingers and toes were eaten by Majok.

Majok ate them whenever he went hunting and failed bagged an animal. When he returned from hunting he asked his wife:

"I failed to bag an animal for food, what I can eat now?"

"If you want to eat me, do so," his wife replied.

"No, my lovely wife, I cannot eat you all, but I will eat one finger so that I can kill my hunger with it tonight," says Majok, and he cut off one finger of his wife with his sharpest teeth. In this way, Majok had eaten all the fingers and toes of his wife over a long space of time until he completely finished them all. So, his wife was staying fingerless and toeless in the house.

When the first wife of Majok saw Akuur, she was upset, and she called her immediately. She was also a daughter of a human being like Akuur.

Hearing his first wife calling his new wife, Majok had been annoyed.

"Why are you calling Akuur?" Majok asked his first wife with the burning dark face. He knew that she would tell Akuur all her secrets about him.

"I want her to come and remove the thorn in my foot', replied the first wife.

"Go and come quickly," Majok said to Akuur.

The first wife told Akuur to sit as if she were removing the thorn from her feet. There was nothing on her feet, it was a trick to tell Akuur all her secrets.

The first wife began telling Akuur the secrets of Majok in low voice: "My sister you came to the wrong place, a place of ruthless Koor, the man-eater Majok Keeror. You look at me, did I come like this from my Father's home? No, I did not come like this, it is Majok who ate all my fingers and toes. When he went out to hunting and he did not find any animal, he comes and eats one of my fingers and my toes. He has been eating them one by one until he finished them like the way you see me now."

Majok bent his head down in order to hear what his wife was murmuring about but he could not hear because the wife spoke with her voice as low as possible.

"What shall I do?" Akuur asked.

"You go back to your home," Majok told her.

"How shall I leave? Will he not eat me?" Akuur asked.

"You will leave as soon as he goes hunting tomorrow," said the first wife. And when you are escaping, you will make up yourself so that no one can recognise you. You will close one of your eyes with mud. You will wear a torn skin. You will walk with a walking stick. You will smoke a broken smoking pipe in your mouth. After you would have left all the dens you will throw away the stick and pipe and run as fast as the wind."

In the following morning Majok left for hunting. Akuur made herself up immediately. She closed one of her eyes with mud, wore a torn apron skin, bore a broken smoking pipe in her mouth. She looked like an old woman. With a walking stick in her hand, she escaped.

On the way, she met Lions, but they thought she was an old woman. After she walked past Lion dens, she threw away all the disguises and she ran as fast as she could.

Majök returned in afternoon. He cut short his hunting in order to come and stay with his new wife, Akuur. When he arrived home, he found Akuur had escaped. He had to throw down the meat and run after her.

When the Adicool the Glossy Starling saw Majok was running, following Akuur. He flew past Majok, reached Akuur and said, "Akuur, run very fast, Majok is running behind following you."

Akuur sped up and ran faster.

Majok stopped and rested in shade under a tree. Adicool saw him and informed Akuur.

"Akuur, Majok is resting."

Akuur went into the shade to rest.

When Majok took off and started running, Adicool saw him and he said, "Akuur, Majok is running."

Akuur started running.

Throughout Akuur's escape, Adicool had been informing her about Majok's running and resting until she reached home, falling down at the home yard, and Majok falling down at the edge of the farm.

Akuur's Father went and brought Majok home.

Akuur was asked by her Father, what the problem was and why they were chasing each other. Akuur said. "Majok Keeror is a Lion, a man-eater who has eaten all the fingers and toes of his first wife and that was the reason, I escaped."

"Were you not told last time," said the Father blaming Akuur, "That dance has a Lion in it. It would have been better if you were eaten by Koor, because you were told but you could not listen."

The Father of Akuur went to Majok too.

"What is the problem, my son?" the Father asked.

"Nothing, there is no problem, I drove the cows to the forest when I returned, I found Akuur had left, so I had to follow her because I did not know where she had gone."

"Since you have said there is no problem, you will go back to your home tomorrow," the Father said.

The Father and the Mother met, slaughtered a goat for daughter, and slaughtered a dog for Majok. The goat and the dog were cooked separately in two different pots.

In the evening the Mother called Akuur to brief about their entertainment with goat and dog meat. She told her that she had cooked a dog for Majok, and she cooked a goat for her. She told her she would put a some small meat and a little soup of dog into two smaller separate bowls. She told Akuur if they would later eat in darkness, and Majok smelled a goat meat, then she, Akuur should give him that dog meat and soup. Then, Akuur returned to the house where they were sitting with Majok.

Then in evening, the Mother brought the dog meat in a pot, and she gave it to Majok, and he started eating it. She returned and brought a goat meat in another pot, and she gave it to Akuur, along with two small bowls of dog meat and soup.

When Akuur was eating, Majok immediately smelled the goat meat. "Akuur my wife," Majok called, "Why does your beef look like goat meat. Is it the same meat as mine?"

"Yes, it is the same meat as yours," Akuur answered.

"Let me taste your meat, Akuur, if it is the same as my meat," Majok said.

Akuur gave him dog meat in a calabash

Majok tasted it and he said, "Good. It is the same meat."

When Akuur was sipping her soup, Majok sniffed the goat soup again.

"Akuur my wife, why is your soup smelling like goat soup?" Majok said.

"It is the same soup as yours," Akuur said.

"Let me taste it," asked Majok.

Akuur gave him dog soup in a small bowl.

Majok tasted it and he said, "It is good, it is the same as mine."

After Majok and Akuur had eaten, they were taken to sleep. A ram was tied down behind the house. At midnight when all the people were sound asleep, Majok transformed himself slowly into a Lion.

"Akuur, I will eat you now," said Majok. "People, your daughter is about to be eaten," cried the ram. Majok the Lion stopped from eating Akuur, and he attacked the ram and ate it. After Majok had eaten the ram, he had threatened to eat Akuur three times but the rope, peg and payrus had been disrupting him until daybreak.

When the day broke, Majok and Akuur left for their home in the morning. Before they set off, the three brothers told Akuur their sister, they would be hiding themselves on the way near the two big tamarind trees in the forest.

When they were walking in the forest, Majok stopped, and asked,"Akuur, which forest is this?"

"It is the forest where our goats graze in," Akuur replied.

Then Majok and Akur went to another forest.

"Which forest is this?" Majok asked.

"It is the forest where our calves graze in," Akur answered.

"It is the forest that our cows graze in,"Akur replied.

They walked and Majok stopped and asked, "It is the forest where the bulls of my brother Deng graze in," Akuur said.

When they arrived at the two tamerind trees, where

Akur's brothers were hiding, Majok stopped and asked, "Akuur, which forest is this?"

"I do not know. How many times have I told you?" Akuur said angrily. He began to throw abusive words at her.

Glossary - Pronunciations

Majok (Majök)
Keroor (Këroor)
Adicool (Adïcol)

Acany
the Lion's Wife

O nce upon a time there lived a woman called Acany, the daughter of a man who was married by a Lion. One day her Mother visited her home. The Mother arrived in afternoon, when Koor the Lion, her husband, had gone hunting. As Koor the Lion had not yet returned from hunting, Acany advised her Mother on how she should behave in Koor's den.

"My Mother," called Acäny, "When my husband comes, he will slaughter a goat for you. When I cook the entrails and I give them to you, do not eat them, give them back to Koor, my husband. When I cook the whole goat and I give it to you, you divide it into two lots: our six parts and their six parts. Among my children, some resemble my husband Koor and they will eat with their Father - thee Lion. Some are human and resemble me, they will eat with us. When you are eating, do not eat all meat on the bones, leave a little meat on the bones and after we finish eating, you will go and throw the bones away. And when you are throwing away the bones, do not throw them in the grass or in water, you throw them in an open area. When you drink your soup, do not drink all the soup, leave a little soup in the calabash and later go and put it in an open area, do not pour it in grass or in water."

"My daughter," agreed the Mother, "This is not a home, it is wilderness, I will do as you say." After Acany finished briefing the Mother, she took her and hid her in the granary so that Koor would not eat her by accident if he arrived in a hurry from hunting.

By the late afternoon, there were shorter and louder calls from the farm. "Acany, my lovely wife, come and take me, come and take the shoulder of meat." Acany ran out, rushing to the farm, it was now Koor who arrived from hunting. Acany lifted up Koor, carrying him into his cattle barn. Acany returned and she carried the shoulder of meat home. It is the habit of a Koor who marries a man's daughter, if he goes to hunt

and he returns, he stops at the farm and he is carried to his stable by his wife. Koor was always being carried either, by the neck, on the back or on the bosom. Koor always eats most of the animal in the forest and brings only the shoulder of meat to his wife and children.

No sooner had Koor sat inside the cattle stable than he smelled something, and came out. He loudly called, "Acany, who came here when I was away?"

"Nobody came here," Acany denied.

"But what smells like human being here?" Koor asked.

"Am I not human being? If you plan to eat me, you can do so," Acany said.

"No, I cannot eat you, my lovely wife," Koor said, "I actually smelled something like human beings, may be some humans are passing in the nearby forest."

Koor returned to the stable. After Koor rested and changed from a wild, forest and hunting mood, to a home and human mood, Acany gave Koor his food. As Koor was eating, Acany told him about her Mother.

"Where is she?" Koor asked.

"She is in granary," replied Acany said.

"Stop your hatred of people who walk on two legs in my home," Koor shouted at Acany, "Why do you hide my Mother-in-law in granary? Acäny! Tell me clearly why did you hide her in the granary? I have always been saying that human beings are bad-natured and envious creatures. I have never witnessed that, and I have witnessed it today. How dare you hide my Mother in-law. If you are not careful Acany, I swear by the grey sky, I will harm you. Bring her out."

Acäny went and brought her Mother out of the granary. After receiving his Mother-in- law happily, Koor ran into the cattle barn, picking a very fat goat. "This is your goat my Mother," Koor said, "I will slaughter it now for you alone. You will eat it alone, do not give even a bone to your daughter's nephews and nieces. And to you Acany and your children, I do not want anyone among you to eat with my Mother; no one must not even watch her when she is eating."

Koor skinned the goat quickly, bringing out the entrails and taking them to Acany, telling her to cook them. Acany cooked them and she took them to her Mother. Her Mother did not eat them, she took them to Koor, her son-in-law, who pretentiously refused, but the Mother-in-law persuaded him until he agreed and ate them.

When the whole goat was cooked, the Mother-in-law divided it into two parts.

One part for the Koor members of the family, and the other part for the human members of the family.

Immediately after the meat was served, the Pride rushed in, ate their meat, grabbing it and quarrelling among themselves and chewing all the bones. While, on the other hand, the human members of the family were eating slowly and leaving a little meat on the bones.

After they had finished eating, Koor the Father came, moving around the human members, watching them with keen interest and much appetite as they were eating.

As soon as the human members finished eating,

Koor the Father jumped in, saying he wanted to throw away their bones. The Mother-in-law denied him, saying she was the one to throw the bones away. The Mother-in-law went and threw the bones in an open area and placed the soup in a calabash nearby them. After the Mother-in-law came home, Koor the Father stole himself to the open area: he drank the soup in the calabash, and he chewed all bones.

After the goat meat of the Mother-in-law's entertainment, the main meat for the family, from hunting, was served. The meat was divided again into two, one for the Pride and the other for humans. Then Acany called her Mother aside and she spoke to her.

"Mother, you are going to cut the meat for my husband, Koor," Acany said, "When you are cutting his meat, you cut first one, very big round piece of meat, so he swallows without chewing it, and then you will cut the rest into pieces as small as you can." The Mother-in-law nodded her head, and he carried the meat to the cattle stable, where the Pride and the children he resembled were. The Mother-in-law satisfactorily cut the meat for Koor, her son-in-law.

When the time came for sleeping. Acany called her Mother aside, she spoke to her on how she should sleep in the cattle stable at night. Acany said, "Mother you are going to sleep in the stable, inside there the cows will step you, will release their dung on you, when the cows do things to you, do not complain." And then Acany gave the butter to her Mother, to smear it on her nose for when the cows would release dung later at night. Acany continued, "You say, why the cows of my daughter produce good dung like this. Their dung has sweetest smell ever." In the stable there were two types of cow, one who had horns and one who had no horns. The horned cows were real cows but the hornless were Lions.

Afterwards, the Mother went to sleep in the stable.

At midnight, a hornless cow stepped on her, piercing her down hard with a hoof. The Mother-in-law strengthened her heart by bearing the pain and keeping silent, and she never said anything.

After sleeping for a while, another hornless cow released dung on her. The Mother-in-law responded, saying, "Why the cows of my daughter have good dung like this? Their dung has the sweetest smell I have ever smelt." The Mother-in-law said that while smearing the butter onto her nose. Actually, the Mother-in-law spent the night, being disgusted by the dung of hornless cows that eat meat, their dung smell like humans. There was no problem with the horned cows who eat grasses, their dung was odourless. When the day broke, the Mother-in-law brought cows out of the barn. She cleaned the stable of the dung. When Koor, her son-in-law woke up, he found the stable had already been cleaned of the dung. So, he went to hunt.

After Koor went hunting, Acany spent with day with Mother. When it was late afternoon there was a shorter and louder call: "Acany, my lovely wife and my Mother-in-law come and take me and come and take the shoulder." Both Acany and her Mother ran out to Koor.

"Acany take the shoulder, my Mother-in-law takes me," said Koor. Acany carried the shoulder of the meat while the Mother lifted up to her chest, the very heavy Koor, who had eaten the whole animal in the forest. She lowered him down and rested. The Mother lifted up Koor to her neck, with a few steps she staggered and lowered him down and rested. Finally, the Mother-in-law lifted up Koor on her back and she carried him in the barn.

When the food was served, Koor told Acany to let his Mother-in-law rest and that his meat should be given to him without a spear because he would use his teeth.

When it was the time for sleeping, Koor told Acany to put his Mother-in-law in the hut, not the stable.

The Mother-in-law slept comfortably in the hut. In the morning the Mother went to Acany and told her, she wanted to go back home. Acany advised her, "If Koor, my husband, asks you what type of cow you want? A horned or hornless cow? You say you need a horned cow."

Then the Mother-in-law went to Koor, and she told him that she would like to leave.

"My Mother-in-law, what cow shall I give you, is it the horned or hornless cow?" Koor asked.

"I am hornless / Can I be given hornless cow again? No, I want a long-horned cow," the Mother-in-law said.

When the Mother-in-law was about to leave with her long-horned cow, Acany called her into the house, and she gave her raw, white cotton.

"Mother, if anyone asks you on the way, 'Where are you bringing the cow?' "You tell him," 'I am bringing the cow from my in-laws,' and if they ask, 'in-laws whose teeth look like what?' You say, 'whose teeth are as white as this cotton, even if this cotton almost fades.'"

After that the grandMother came out and she took the ashes, blowing it onto the feet of her grandchildren.The grandMother also scooped the water in the smallest calabash, spitting saliva into it, then sprinkling this upon the children as a blessing. "Those who once meet, always meet," said the Mother-in-law and she left immediately, without glancing lest she withdrew the blessing.

The Mother-in-law was now pulling her horned cow by the rope. Accompanying her behind the cow was Koor, her son-in-law. As they were moving through Koor village, someone came up and stood near the footpath.

"Woman" he asked, "Where you are bringing the cow from?"

"I am bringing the cow from my in-laws," the Mother-in-law said.

"In-laws whose teeth look like what?" he asked.

"An in-laws whose teeth are as white as this cotton and even this cotton is almost faded, compared to their teeth," the Mother-in-law said.

"Alright, you go, your cow is beautiful," he said.

Who was this unknown person? Some Lions who are relatives of Acany's husband were looking for a way to eat Acany's Mother.

The Mother-in-law arrived in another village. Another unknown person came up and stood near the footpath.

"Woman," he asked, "Where are you bringing the cow from?"

"I am bringing the cow from my in-laws," the Mother-in-law said.

"In-laws, whose teeth look like what?" he asked.

"In-laws whose teeth are as white as this cotton. Even this cotton fades, compared to their teeth," the Mother-in-law said.

"Alright, you go, your cow is beautiful," he said.

After they had reached the end of Koor's territory, her son-in-law returned and the Mother-in-law drove her cow to her human home.

When Acany's Father saw Acany's mother bringing a cow from Acany's home, he said he would also bring a cow. In the morning the Father left for Acany's home. The Father arrived in the afternoon when Koor, the husband of Acany, had not yet come from hunting in the forest. The Father stood in the farm. Acany killed a cock on the line separating the home floor from the farmland, and the Father jumped over the cock. Acany told her Father, if her husband were there, he would have welcomed him with a bull. The Father sang a divine song to his daughter and his grandchildren, spitting saliva on their heads as a blessing.

Before Koor would arrive from hunting, Acany advised her Father on how he should wisely behave. "My Father," said Acany, "When my husband comes, he will kill for you a goat. When I cook the entrails of the goat and I give them to you, do not eat them. Give them back to Koor, my husband. When I cook the whole goat and I give it to you, you divide it into two different lots: our six parts and their six parts. The children are from Koor's lineage, they resemble the Lion. They will eat with Koor, their Father. Some are humans, they resemble me, and they will eat with us. When you are eating, do not eat all meat on the bones, leave a little meat on them. When we finish eating, you will go to throw the bones in an open area, do not throw them in grass or in water. When you drink the soup, do not drink the soup all, leave a little soup in the calabash. You will put down that little soup in an open area, do not pour it in the grass or in water. Last word, Koor, my husband has not a hand to hold a spear to cut his meat, and he cannot use his teeth at home to eat like he does in the forest. So, you are going cut his meat for him and his children. When you are cutting his meat, you first cut one big piece of meat and give it to him so that he masticates it and then you cut the rest of the meat into as many small pieces as possible."

"Is that all? I know all this?" the Father said.

After the briefing Acany took her Father into the granary to hide him, so that Koor will not eat him by mistake when he arrives hurriedly and wild from hunting. No sooner, in the granary, the Father was crying of hotness and sweat. "Acany, open the granary, so I come out, the heat is almost killing me," shouted the Father.

"No, you wait in the granary until Koor returns," Acany said.

Suddenly, something was thrown down heavily, and there was a shorter and louder call from the farm. "Acany, come and take me and come and take the shoulder of meat," Koor said.

Acäny first ran to the granary and told her Father to keep quiet, that Koor had arrived and then she proceeded to the farm, lifted up Koor, carrying him to his cattle stable, then returning, brought the shoulder home.

As Koor was sitting inside the stable, Koor smelled something and he came out.

"Acany, who came here when I was away?" Koor asked.

"No one came here," Acany denied.

"But what thing is giving out a smell like a human being here?" Koor asked.

"But am I not a human being? If you plan to eat me, you can," Acany said.

'No, I cannot eat you my lovely wife," Koor said. "But there is something that smelled like man," Koor said and returned his stable.

Acany gave food to Koor. As he was eating, his emotions cooled down, changed from wild hunting mood to a home one, then Acany told him about her Father.

"Where is he?" Koor asked.

"He is in the granary," Acany replied.

"Go quickly and bring him out."

Acany brought her Father out of the granary.

Koor went to the herd of goats picked out a fat goat. "This is your goat," Koor said. "I am going to prepare it now for you alone. You will eat it alone, do not give even a bone to the children of your daughter. To you Acany and your children I do not want anyone of you to eat with my Father-in-law, no one must watch him, even eating."

Shortly, Koor brought entrails and he told Acany to cook them quickly for his important guest. Acany cooked them and she took them to her Father.

The Father forgot what Acany told him as he ate entrails. When the Father-in-law was eating, Koor was watching him with saliva slobbering down from his mouth. After the Father-in-law had finished eating entrails, Koor stood up from where he was lying and watching. He stretched himself and his stomach rumbled loudly, he went back to his cattle barn.

When the whole goat was cooked, the Father-in-law divided it into two. Koor members were given their six parts and humans were given six parts as well. Each group started eating. The human members of the family were eating slowly and quietly, while the Pride were eating noisily, grabbing the meat, and quarrelling among themselves. After the Pride finished, Koor came to move around where the human members of the family were still eating to watch them. When the Father-in-law saw him, he was angry and shouted, "What is this now? Why do you come to watch the eyes of people when people are eating? You will let the meat choke the people."

When Koor heard these blistering words, he felt ashamed. He went back to his cattle barn, lay down with his forelegs stretched forward and watched the humans eating through an open door of the barn. When the Father-in-law was eating, he was eating all the meat on the bones. He was forgetting what his daughter told him; to leave a little meat on the bones. After the human members finished their food, Koor the Father made a long jump from the stable, landing in the middle between the cattle barn and house, and trotted to the door. He was going to take the bones and pour them.

"No," refused the Father-in-law, "I will pour them out myself." The Father-in-law walked to the edge of the farm and he poured the bones in a pond of water and splashed the soup on the grass, forgetting what his daughter told him.

After the Father-in-law went back home, Koor the

son-in-law stole himself to the pond, he found the bones thrown in the water and the soup splashed on the grasses. Koors's stomach rumbled loudly, snorting out some words through his nose. Koor entered the water, collecting up the bones with his claws. Koor came out of the water and he also turned to the grass, licking up the soup on the grasses.

In the evening, the meat from hunting was now served as the night's food. This meat was cooked in two separate pots. The meat for the Pride of the family was cooked whole, not cut into pieces, while the meat of the human members was cut into pieces. When the food for the night was ready, Acany called her Father aside, she advised him on how he should cut the meat of Koor.

"Father, I told you two things before and you forgot them, when you are cutting his meat," explained Acany, "You cut first a very big one round piece of meat so that Koor can swallow it without chewing , and then you cut the rest of meat into as many small pieces as possible."

"Stop talking, I know. Why do you advise me like a child?" Father-in-law asked.

The Father-in-law went to cut the meat for Koor, his son-in-law. He cut the whole meat into small pieces, forgetting what his daughter told him. Koor picked a small piece of meat, masticating it. The meat flew into his hollow stomach, falling to the backside. The small pieces of the meat were slipping out through Koor's backside because there was not big one piece of meat to block the backside. The first big one round piece was always meant to block the backside of Koor. As Koor was eating, the meat kept falling through his anus. His children ran behind him and began picking up the pieces of meat that were falling from his backside. "We are picking from our Father's backside," said the children joyously. Koor was very angry, but he controlled himself.

When it was a time for sleeping, Acany called her Father aside and she told him, "Father, you going to sleep in the stable. When a cow steps on you, do not complain because some of them are Lions. When a cow releases dung on you, do not complain because of those cows are Lions. When a cow releases dung you say, 'Why the cows of my daughter have very good dung.' Take this butter to smear it on your nose."

"Stop talking I know all this," said the Father, "Why do you advise me as I were a child?"

When the Father-in-law was going to sleep in the stable, he threw away the butter before entering the stable.

At midnight a hornless cow stepped a sharp hoof on the father-in-law, trampling him hard. The father- in-law cried and chanted his slogan. He woke up, still sleepy and hit his walking stick in the darkness, beating the cow's thigh. The cow's stomach rumbled loudly, snorting out through the nose some angry words.

After the Father-in-law had fallen asleep again, another hornless cow released dung on him. He had woken up and still sleepy he hit a stick in the darkness, he had missed the cow. All the cows had run and hid behind the wall.

Realizing the Father-in-law was beating nothing in the darkness, the hornless cows murmured; laughing in low snorting voices.

"Laugh and you laugh at what my heart hates," said the Father, "Look at your red curved teeth as if they were the teeth of the blood suckers."

Early in the morning, the Father-in-law woke up, got out of the stable and went and sat very far away in the farm. The Father-in-law never brought the cows out of the cattle barn and he never cleaned it. When Koor, his son in law woke up, he saw him sitting very far in the farm, and was very angry because the home was smelling bad. Koor looked at him with bad eyes but kept silent and he left for hunting.

In the late afternoon, suddenly, something was thrown down heavily, and there was a shorter and louder call from the farm.

"Acany my lovely wife and my Father-in-law come and take me and come and take the shoulder."

Both went to Koor, Acany ran quickly while her Father was walking slowly.

"Acany take the shoulder! My Father-in-law takes me," Koor said.

Acany took the shoulder home. The Father lifted up Koor by both hands to his chest. Carrying him, he teetered for few steps then stopped, lowered him down and rested. The Father-in-law lifted him on his back again, teetering with him, finally throwing him down heavily in the cattle camp, "How can you eat too much and yet force me to carry you?" the Father-in-law said.

When the time came for sleeping, the Father-in-law refused to sleep in the stable, he went to sleep in the goat shed. In the morning the Father-in-law said he wanted to leave. Acany told him that he should tell her husband the Lion, and she also advised her Father, if Koor asked him, which type of cow he would like to be given, whether it was horned or hornless cow, he should take the horned cow.

"Do not tell me, I know," said the Father who went straight to Koor and he told him he would like to leave.

"What type of cow shall I give you, is it hornless or longhorned cow?"

"Can my wife take a longhorned cow and I take a longhorned cow too?" said the Father. "I want the hornless cow."

Koor gave a hornless cow to him.

When the Father-in-law was about to leave, Acany called him inside the house, and she gave him raw white cotton.

"Father, if anyone asks you on the way, 'Where are you bringing the cow from?' Acany explained, "You tell them, 'I am bringing the cow from my in-laws.' If they ask, 'In-laws whose teeth look like what?' You say, 'Whose teeth are as white as this cotton, even when this cotton almost fades compared to their teeth."

"I know, do not tell me," said the Father-in-law and he took the white cotton. He drove out his cow and beat it terribly with a stick. His son-in-law came and said, "You pull it." The Father-in-law pulled the cow by the rope, with Koor, his son-in-law now escorting him. As they were walking, an unknown person appeared, stood by the footpath.

"You man, where you are bringing the cow?" he asked.

"I am bringing the cow from my in-laws," the Father-in-law said.

"From in-laws whose teeth look like what?" he asked again.

The Father-in-law threw away the white cotton, ran into near bushes, plucked out reddest flower and in loudest voice said, "My in-laws have the reddest teeth like this flower. Their teeth are as red as if they suck blood. And more about them they are…"

"Enough, you go. Your cow is beautiful," the strange man interrupted him from continuing to say more words.

When the father-in-law picked up the rope of the cow and pulled it, the cow stood still. He pulled it strongly and the cow jumped up landing its sharp hoof on his heel, injuring him severely. The blood was like water. Seeing the blood, the Father-in-law turned around, with black eyes and fury, he cruelly flogged the cow with a stick. The cow jumped violently up, and swung its neck up and down, almost slipping out of the Father-in-law's hands but he held the rope tightly. After cooling down, the cow's stomach rumbled heavily, roaring out some angry words through the nose.

The Father-in-law walked a few paces. Someone came out.

"You man, where you are bringing the cow?" he asked.

"From my in-laws," the Father in law said.

"Whose teeth look like what?" he asked.

"Whose teeth are red as blood? And they have the

ugliest gums I ever saw and have the baddest smelling mouth ever," the Father said.

"Enough, take your cow, your cow is beautiful," he said.

When the Father-in-law had passed all the villages of the Pride, the son-in-law said he was going back home. The Father-in-law was now walking alone into the bush. The cow started transforming itself into Koor; its short teeth grew into the long teeth of a Lion and its hooves into claws. The cow suddenly sprang up, slipping out of the rope in the Father-in-law's hands. Under a nearby tree it walked back like a ram, knocking its head on the tree and became a Lion. Suddenly, leaping like a frog, he broke the neck of the Father-in-law.

Shortly, Koor, Acany's husband appeared, and they started eating him. After they had eaten most of the father-in-law, Koor took his groin home.

"Acany, Acany, the wife of my Father's cows, cook for me this groin," Koor snorted.

Acany examined the groin, recognising them as her Father. "They have eaten my Father, god let me revenge my Father," she mourned quietly inward. Acany mixed up the red pepper and sand, filling them without cutting them into pieces, she cooked them. When Acany was cooking, she poorly lit the fire under the pot. As a result of less fire, they remained raw as much of it never cooked. At the time Acany was cooking she was also cooking three other pots of food.

Then Acany took the un-cooked groins to Koor in the stable. Koor picked one, which he bit with his teeth and pulling it with his hands. It had ruptured, spilled the sand and the red pepper into Koor's eyes. Koor wailed, "Acany bring me water quickly because sand has poured into my eyes."

Acany came, said, "long ago in our home, if something like that spilled into someone's eyes, the peelings of willow tree's fruit were put in the mortar and the person would place his face in the mortar and it is washed with water."

"Go to light it quickly," Koor said.

Acany kindled the fire with peelings, held Koor by the hands, took him to the mortar, bent his face down, and she left him to bring the water. But instead of bringing the water, she brought the pestle and she beat the neck of the Lion. With the sand and pepper in his eyes, Koor grasped Acany but he missed her because was not seeing. Acany continued hitting his neck until he fell down. And finally, Acany beat him to death.

As the Lion was laying dead on the floor, Acany took the three pots of food, and she placed each pot on each three footpaths coming home. Then Acany burned both the cattle barn and the house. Acany also threw the children who resembled the Lion onto the fire, and she left with the children who resembled her.

When she was leaving, she met some Lions on the way.

"Acany, what is that smoke coming out of your home?" one of the Lions asked.

"I do not know, but it may be the smoke from Timgaar cattle camp," said Acieny.

When the small baby on Acany's back in apron skin, who resembled the Lion, heard it, he said, "No, it is not, the smoke is from Acany who hit my Father's neck with the pestle and burned our home."

"Acany, what is the child saying?" asked one of suspicious Lions who half-way heard what the child said.

"The child is sick, and I am taking him to a Magician," said Acany.

Behind at home, when the nearby Lions saw the smoke, they came to see what was happening. Before they would reach home, they found the food on footpath that Acany had left and they sat and started eating it. Another group of Lions came in from the other path. They found the food and they sat and started eating. The Pride who came to see what was happening, sat down and started eating the food before they could see what exactly was happening. After all the

Lions had finished eating the food, they came home, finding their brother was killed by Acany. The Pride became furious and angry with Acany. They started to chase Acany.

Vowing to capture Acany and bite her with long fangs before they threw her on fire, like she threw the children on fire, they kept chasing Acany. At that time, the Lions set off to chase Acany. Acany had already gone very, very, very far because the Lions were delayed by eating the food before they could come home and see what Acany did. Lions were running, running, running …

As the Pride were coming, Acany reached the river that divided the pride's village from the human village. Acany prayed, "If you were the river of my grandparents, dry up, may I never touch your fish or your seashells."

The river dried up immediately and all seashells and fishes remained on the river bed. Acany crossed the river, and the water returned into the river.

On the other side of the river, Acany sat in shade of the tree to rest.

Then Lions arrived hurriedly with their big hairy mouths, breathing heavily, "Acany," they called snorting through their noses, "How did you cross the river?"

"I crossed the river by saying," Acany said, "If you are a river of my grandparents, you dry up, never will I touch your catch of fish, never will I touch your seashells."

"If you are my grandparents' river, you dry up and never will we touch your fishes, never will we touch your seashells."

The river dried up. All the fishes and seashells remained very fat on the river floor. The Lions descended into the river floor, when the Pride saw the fishes, they started to eat fishes. The water began to come back.

A member of the Pride saw the water and said, "My brothers we shall drown; the water is coming."

Another Lion replied, "Let's ...eat, we shall cough the water out." The water came in, suddenly washing away all the Lions and drowning them. The small child who was on Acany's back saw them crying in water. It also cried, "My uncles are drowning."

Acany seized him by the legs, spinning him over her head, throwing him into the water, and the child drowned. Acany and other children went to the human village.

Biok Yom

A man was walking on the footpath through a village. The Woman saw him and she ran after him calling out, "Biok Yom, the son of my mother, where are you going and where are you coming from?"

"I am coming from our family home you left a long time ago," he said.

The man was tricking her. He was not actually her brother, he was not actually called Biok Yom but because the woman called him like that, he accepted the name.

The Woman took him to her home. She told her children that their uncle Biok Yom had come. However, her children were afraid of Biok Yom because he had grown too much hair on his head.

"Mother, why does our uncle have long hair? Why does he look strange?" one of the children asked, "We are afraid of him."

The Woman told her children he was their real, maternal uncle. She said she would shave his hair as soon as possible. She went and brought a razor blade, called Biok Yom and started to shave his head: Murë ë Köör ë nhom.[1]

As she was shaving Biok Yom's hair, the hair was continuously growing. As soon as it was shaved it immediately grew again. When she finished shaving one side of the head and she moved to shave the other side, the hair grew immediately in the part she had finished. As the Woman was shaving and the hair grew, one of children asked again, "Mother, why is the hair of our uncle continuously growing so quickly after it is shaved?"

"It is because his hair has not been shaved for a very long time," the Woman answered.

After she had been shaving him for the whole day, and the hair had continued to grow again immediately where she had just shaved, the Woman became tired and stopped shaving. "Biok Yom, the son of my mother, I am going to cook, I will shave your hair later in the evening," the Woman said.

In the evening after cooking, she started to shave

again until the sun went down. She continued shaving until midnight but the hair kept growing. She told Biok Yom she would resume shaving on the following day and she slept. In the morning Biok Yom said he wanted to leave.

The Woman thanked him for his visit, and she said she was very sorry that she had not finished shaving his hair, but she would when he returned next time.

When the man was leaving, the Woman gave him one of her daughters. They reached a thick and dark forest where no man's sound was heard, only the chirruping of the birds and crying of the wild animals was heard.

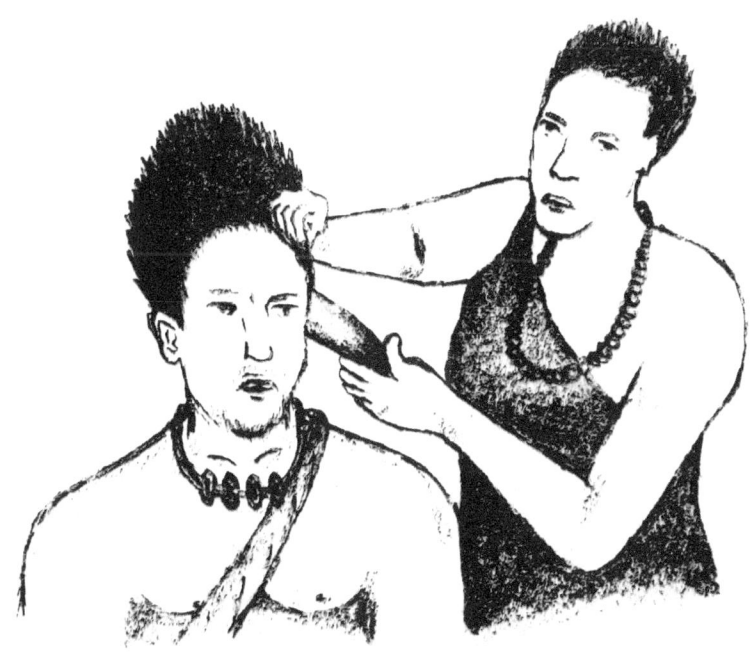

Biok Yom stopped and bent down and he showed his backside to the girl.

"Young girl, can you smell my backside, does it smell as I am your real, maternal uncle or does it smell like I am someone else?" Biok Yom asked.

"It smells like my real maternal uncle, not like a stranger," the Daughter said after smelling the backside. She was now afraid. She knew he was not her uncle, an uncle would not ask her to do such a thing.

"Let us go," Biok Yom said.

Biok Yom and the Daughter arrived at his home. The Daughter found that Biok Yom was not a human being but a Lion; a Man-eater whose home was full of human skulls and bones.

At Biok Yom's house, the wife of Biok Yom looked at the Daughter as if she was her own granddaughter, as if she was her Grandmother.

Grandmother gave sorghum to her Granddaughter to pound in the mortar. When she was pounding the sorghum in the mortar, it began to speak. The Mortar knew that the the man-eater was going to kill the girl. But the Mortar did not want to say this aloud. He tried to warn her quietly, "Girl, you are breaking me up. The sorghum flour will be used to season you." As the Girl pounded with pestle, the Pestle also spoke to her quietly. The Pestle said, "Girl, you are breaking me up. The sorghum flour will be used to season you."

"What do the Mortar and Pestle mean by saying all these things? How will I be spiced and seasoned with sorghum flour?" the Girl asked herself. The Girl realised that she was going to be eaten. She hurriedly pounded the sorghum and took the flour to the Grandmother. As soon as she gave Grandmother the flour, she was sent to wash the calabashes in the pond on the edge of the farm.

At the pond, the Girl picked up a frog in the water and she asked him, "Aguek the Frog, I am going to escape. How will you answer when Grandmother calls for me?"

"I will croak as usual," Aguek said.

"You are not my Aguek," the Girl said and threw the frog away. She picked another and asked him, "Aguek, how will you answer after I have escaped and Grandmother calls me?"

"I will answer, 'Yes, my Grandmother, I am coming,'" Aguek said.

"Good, Aguek. Thank-you," the Girl said. Then she jumped up and fled, running to her own home where she had left her mother.

Grandmother waited, but the Granddaughter did not arrive and so she called;

"My granddaughter, are you coming?"

"Yes, my Grandmother, I am coming,"Aguek said.

The Grandmother kept quiet, and waited for a while and then she called out again;

"My Granddaughter, are you coming?"

"Yes, my Grandmother I am coming,"Aguek answered.

"Bring the calabashes, the food is ready."

But thanks to Aguek, the Girl was already half way to her home.

After the Grandmother had been waiting for a long time, and the Granddaughter had not come, she went herself to the pond and found that it was Aguek the Frog who was answering her. When the Aguek saw her coming, it jumped into water.

The Grandmother ran to her husband to inform him that the Grandaughter had escaped. He jumped up quickly to chase her, running as fast as wind. No sooner had the Girl arrived at her home she saw Biok Yom had arrived too. He told the Girl's mother that she had run away from him.

The Woman shouted at her and said, "If you do not like to stay with Biok Yom, my brother, I will go myself to stay with him."

"It is a bad home, littered with human bones and skulls in the yard, the Girl murmured to her siblings,

"How can she not see that he is not her brother?"

Then the Woman left with Biok Yom, and her children remained in their home alone.

When Biok Yom and the Woman arrived at his home, the Woman was immediately given a big basket full of sorghum to pound in the mortar. As she was pounding the sorghum in the mortar, the Mortar spoke to her, "Woman, you are breaking me up. The sorghum flour will be used to season you." As she pounded with the pestle, the Pestle also spoke to her, "Woman, you are breaking me up. The sorghum flour will be used to season you."

The Mortar and the Pestle warned the Woman, but the Woman did not understand what they were telling her.

After the pounding of the sorghum, the Woman brought the flour and she gave it to the wife of Biok Yom.

"Woman," called Biok Yom with eyes burning like the eyes of a Lion, "Put the big pot on the fire and fill the water to the top, do not fill it low, fill it to the top. When the water has boiled, call me. I am plaiting a rope for the cow inside the stable."

The Woman filled the water to the top and after the water had boiled and it was very hot, the Woman called Biok Yom.

The Man-eater came out of the cattle byre with a new grey rope, and moving like the wind, made the rope into a noose and threw it around the Woman's neck. Closing it, he pulled her down violently until she rolled on the ground like a sausage tree fruit. Dragging her around the cattle byre, he pronounced to his divinity that he was offering a sacrifice, not a bull, but a big, fat, black woman.

Whining like a lost dog, the Woman tried to reach the helping hand of Jok, but it was out of reach. She pleaded for mercy;

"Biok Yom, my brother, do not kill me," she begged.

'When were we born?" the Man-eater shouted and lifting her up, threw her into the boiling water.

"You will die now. Never again will you find a stranger on a path and call him your brother."

The hot water burned off the skin of the Woman, peeling it red. As she bitterly shed tears into the boiling water, the Man-eater was chanting and evoking his gods to accept his offering of the fat woman.

Glossary

[1]Murë ë Köör ë nhom is the shaving of the Lion's head. It is a famous Dinka proverb derived from the Biok Yom fable.

Abil-Thiang the Chief's Daughter

Once upon a time there was a daughter of a chief called Abil-Thiäng. One afternoon, Abil-Thiäng and other girls, went to look for and eat berries and cherries of different trees in the forest. When the rain poured they ran into the byre of a certain man, to take cover from the rain. When the rain stopped, the girls thanked the man and stood up to leave. The man, the owner of byre, jumped and sat in the doorway.

"No one is leaving. Go back," said the man as he changed into a Lion.

The girls stopped and returned, huddling together

in the byre. After the girls had been siting for a long time and the sun had set, one girl stood up, and she went to the Lion:

"Let me leave alone, it's getting dark," begged the girl.

"Who will remain with me if you leave?" asked the Lion.

"You will remain with Abil-Thiang, the daughter of the chief," said the girl.

The Lion allowed her to leave.

Another girl came to Lion. "Big one, let me leave alone, it is getting dark," she said.

"Who will remain with me?" asked the Lion.

"You will remain with Abil-Thiang, the daughter of the chief," said the girl

"Who is Abil-Thiang among you, I can let you go all and there will be no Abil-Thiang at the end," asked the Lion.

The girls pointed her out: "This is Abil-Thiang, the daughter of the chief."

When the Lion saw Abil-Thiang, he allowed all the girls to leave.

When the girls were leaving byre, Abil-Thiang told them, "You go my sisters, I will remain with the Lion. The children of the same mother don't die the same day. And do not tell my Father where you left me because his heart will stop."

As soon as the girls left, the Lion broke the neck of Abil-Thiang, eating her.

The girls came to the cattle camp, and told the Father of Abil-Thiang what had happened.

The Father of Abil-Thiang ran to the Magician that night. He was gived the thorny branches of the Tree of Death. The Magician told him to use the branches to fence the pond of water, where all animals drink in the forest.

In the morning the Father of Abil-Thiang went over and he fenced the pond of the water with branches of Tree of Death. Then he sat in the shade under the tree. The thorny branches were very, very, very dangerous things. If you touch them you die. If they pierce your feet, you die. No one touches it unless it is the one who gives it and the one given it.

The Father had been sitting at the pond for a long space of time, passing the whole morning and afternoon and no animals came. When the sun was bending, the animals began arriving, finding the fence of the thorny branches of the Tree of Death. It had been strongly built around the pond.

The Buffalo was the first who came. He stood far away and asked, "Who fenced the water of big people?"

"I am the one," said the Father of Abil-Thiang.

"Why?" asked the Buffalo.

"My daughter was eaten yesterday by the animals."

"Who ate your daughter exactly?"

"I don't know but I want to know now," said the Father of Abil-Thiang.

The buffalo coughed, vomiting the grass he ate on the previous day: "This is my grass that I ate yesterday," said the Buffalo, "Is your daughter in it?"

The Father of Abil-Thiang searched it and said, "No, she is not in it."

"Therefore, you remove the fence so that I drink."

"I will not remove the fence until my daughter is brought and put to my hands," swore the Father of Abil -Thiang

Then came Elephant the Big.

"Who fenced the water of big people?" asked the Elephant.

"I am the one," said Father of Abil-Thiang.

"Why?"

"My daughter was eaten yesterday by animals."

The Elephant coughed, vomiting the grass he ate the previous day.

"Look this my grass I ate yesterday," said the elephant, "Check if your daughter is in it."

The Father of Abil-Thiang searched it and said, "No, my daughter is not there."

The Giraffe, Antelope, Rhino, Leopard and all other

animals came and coughed, vomiting the grasses they had eaten on the previous day. Abil-Thiang was not found in them.

At last, came the Lion:

"Who fenced the water of big people?" asked the Lion.

"I am the one," said Father of Abil-Thiang.

"Why?"

"My daughter was eaten yesterday by animals."

When the Lion heard this, he shook his mane in grief. "This is very bad, I cried so hard for the death of your daughter, I cried blood" said the Lion, "However, what can we do? Nothing. As the proverb says, let it go. I console you by saying, let it go and God will give your wife three more daughters."

"I don't like and I don't want three more daughters who are not yet born," declared the Father of Abil-Thiang. "And if the animals can't bring her, all animals will die of thirst. It is upon the animals to bring my daughter, or they die."

The Lion was told to vomit what he ate the previous day but he refused. As the Lion was talking with the Father of Abil-Thiang. Fox was shouting behind, provoking and mocking the situation.

"We shall see today who is biggest and mightiest in the forest, some have been saying it is the Lion and some say it is the Elephant," shouted the Fox.

"Lion, vomit what you ate yesterday," said the Father of Abil-Thiang.

"I don't vomit,"said the Lion

"Look all animals," shouted the Fox, "The Lion is delaying the Elephant to drink. Please Lion, vomit what you had eaten yesterday. You are the only person, who has not been searched."When the Elephant saw the Lion was lagging, he plodded out of the shade to the brim of the pond, where the Father of Abil-Thiang and Lion were arguing.

"Lion, you vomit what you ate yesterday?" said the Elephant in a forceful voice and covering the Lion with its mammoth shade.

With the red eyes and black face, the Lion looked up at the Elephant and he was trembling with anger and bravery.

The Fox was still shouting, irritating and trying to set off the Elephant against the Lion if he should not vomit.

"Fox, I cannot vomit to see what happened" the Lion said, glancing behind to the Fox. "I can fight you and your Elephant now."

"I am the one talking to you not the Fox,"said the Elephant in a fighting voice.

Finally, the Lion realized the Elephant was losing his temper, so he vomited and the hand of Abil-Thiang with two fingers, half-chewed, were found in what he had eaten the day before.

There was sudden giggling at the Lion from all animals.

In shame, the Lion agreed to create and bring Abil-Thiang. As the Lion was creating Abil-Thiang, the Animals told the Father of Abil-Thiang to clean up the pond. They told him, "If one thorn pierce anyone's feet and he dies, your daughter will not be created."

The Father of Abil-Thiang started cleaning up the pond of animals from the Tree of Death. After he removed the fence completely, he was given his daughter Abil-Thiang.

Guoot Mabeek:
The Finest Man

O nce upon a time there lived the most handsome man on the land. His name was Guoot Mabeek. He was the leader of the cattle camp youth. He was well known for the parading and stroking of his brightly-coloured, black and white bull whom he had composed excellent, sonorous songs about. He was not yet married. A Lioness met him in several occasions and dances and she felt a desire to eat him, but it was very difficult, because he was always carrying four spears, a shield and a big ebony stick.

To get him, the Lioness transformed itself into a charming girl. And one afternoon, when the sun was in the middle earth, the charming girl passed through the cattle camp. Mabeek Guut saw her and he followed her into trees. He asked her name, the Girl told him her name. She also asked Guoot's name, Guoot told her his name. As they were slowly walking, they held a sweetest conversation about love, songs, dance, bravery, wisdom and cunning, hunting the buffaloes and elephant, fighting the wars... etc. After they had walked away far from the camp, where they could not hear cows bellowing, Guoot told the Girl that he would go back. The girl begged him;

"No, my ostrich's feather," the Girl called Guoot, glorifying him by different nicknames, "Can you accompany me to that near place?"

Looking at her smiling beautifully, Guoot agreed gently, and he accompanied her to the place she said. They reached it.

"My egg of a different bird," Guoot called girl, "Can I go back here?"

"No, can you accompany me to those trees?" asked the girl.

Guoot said, "There are Lions who eat people here, if you want me to accompany you, let me go back to bring my spears, shield and ebony and I will accompany you wherever you want, but now I cannot go there with nothing in my hands."

"Do you just want something to carry in your hands?" she asked.

"Yes," he answered, "I want a thing to carry in my hands. In this forest, there are many Cannibals and Lions."

"Do not be afraid, a brave man like you, doesn't fear. Why am I not fearing when I am a woman? Look when you go back later, I will walk alone in this thick deep forest. I know men believe in things. This is when they are comfortable. I will get for you something to carry," she explained.

The Girl went into grasses, she broke a long grass, husking off the leaves on it and she gave it to Guoot, saying, "This is your spear."

With a smile Guoot took the spear of grass. Walking for a while, they came to the trees and the girl said, "The cattle camp had remained very far, so I can go back here." Guoot said in a tired tone.

Suddenly, Guoot saw the Girl was running violently to a tree, and he was quickly lost in the dust she stirred up by her feet. Guoot stood wondering and confused as to why the Girl was running like that. And there was a loud sound; the Girl knocked her head on the tree,immediately transforming herself into the Koor, the Lioness. She turned, running into Guoot who stood steadily.

"Are you a Lioness?" Guoot calmly asked her, "I am not afraid of you. I am not regretting my death, the only thing I regret is because there is no one to tell the story of my

bravery at the time you eat. I am eaten and I never run, I am eaten, and I never cry."

The Koor flew in the air like the eagle attacking a Prey. The claws of its forelegs pierced Guoot's shoulders and its claws of his hindlegs pierced Guoot's knees. He had fallen heavily backward, and the Lion dragged his body into her home. When Guoot didn't come that afternoon, his friends thought he had mysteriously disappeared. They searched for him in a big man hunt in the forest, but he was never found.

The Koor ate Guoot Mabeek and she threw away all his bones but she kept the skull and arm-bone. She used the arm-bone to bar the mat that hung in the doorway. She also swung the skull of Guoot's head among the milk gourds she hung on the roof of her house.

And she composed two songs in remembering and celebrating her eating of Guoot Mabeek. The first was a women's dance song and the second was a sacred song. The woman's song was called Guoot Mabeek, The Tasteful

Guoot Mabeek, The Tasteful

I ate Guoot Mabeek
Who was so big like elephant?
I ate Guoot Mabeek
Who was so tasty?

The daughters of Mabeek
Are crying
In the herd of cows

I ate Guoot Mabeek
The finest man on the land
The daughters of Mabeek
Will mourn him forever

The sacred song Koor the Lioness sang to evoke his magic was called My arm-bone of Guoot Mabeek.

My arm-bone of Guoot Mabeek
I will use it to bar my door
I will not use a wooden bar
To bar my door

My arm-bone of Guoot Mabeek
I will use it to bar my door
I will bar my door with it
In dry and wet seasons
And in all seasons.

These songs about the eating of Guoot Mabeek were well known in the villages. They were sung in dances and feasts all over by both animals and human beings. It was only in Guoot's camp that they had not yet reached.

One day the Adicool, the Glossy Starling, came over to the Koor and she asked her to sing the song of Guoot Mabeek because, according to her, the songs were so sweet, and she liked them very much. Adicool said she had a child whom he could lull with the songs as its lullaby.

The Koor proudly sang the songs to her. Adicool learnt the song very well, and she went to the cattle ccamp and perched on a dry wood pole where gourds for Guoot's herd of cows were hanging. She sang the songs pleasantly. The sister of Guoot heard the song and she asked the Adicool where she learnt the song from.

"Where did you hear these songs?" asked the sister of Guoot.

"I learnt them from the Koor the Lioness."

The sister of Guoot called the people of the cattle camp to come to hear what the Adicool was saying. All people came and the bird was asked to sing the songs. He sang the song very well.

"Where did you hear this song?" asked the sister of Guoot.

'I heard and learnt it from the Lion in village,' said the Adicool, the Glossy Starling.

"Can you go and show us that village?" asked the People.

"Yes," said Adicool.

When the youth were about to go to the home of Koor, some people began to doubt the words of Adicool, whether he was telling the truth or a lie.

"Adicool," called one of the people, "How much shall we surely know that you are telling the truth and lying?"

"If you think, I am lying," said the Adicool, "Then I will lie down on the cattle-path tomorrow and all cows will trample me. If I am lying the cow will kill me. If I am not lying, I will remain alive."

People agreed and in the morning Adicool lay down on cattle-path. All the cows walked on it and after all the cows passed over it, he got up and he sang thesongs of Guoot Mabeek.

People slept again without going to Koor.

In following morning, when youth were about to go to the Lion's home, other people still said what the bird was saying was false and there was no need to go to the Lion, they said the stampeding of the bird by cows should not be proof.

"If you think I am lying, you put me in a heap of dry cow dung, you set it on fire, if am lying I will burn to death. If I am telling the truth, I will come out of the fire alive."

The Adicool was put inside a fire of cow dung. Adicool slept in the cow dung fire. In the morning it came out alive, singing the song of Guoot. Then the people believed what the bird was saying was true.

The youth of cattle, with hotly sharpened spears and shields, went to the Lions' village. At early morning, while still dark, the youth had hidden themselves in the grass around the edge of the farm of the Lioness.

After the sun rose, Adicool the Glossy Starling went to the Lion.

'My friend Lioness," Adicool said, "I forgot the song of Guoot Mabeek, can you sing it for me for the last time?"

"Why do you always forget it?" asked the Lioness, "How many times have I been singing it to you? How many times do you want me to sing it to you? I am tired."

"The song is so sweet to me, my baby likes it so much," said the Adicool. "If you sing it to me this time, I swear I will not forget again."

The Koor the Lioness happily sang the songs. No sooner had she finished singing the song to the Adicool, the cattle camp youth and the brothers of Guoot came out of hiding. The Lioness begged that they should not kill her, but they should allow her to create for them their Guoot Mabeek, as the most handsome, as ever before. The Lioness went to the forest to collect the bones and she proceeded to the house of the Creator, to bring other things for creating. After she brought all the things, she went into the house, closing herself in the house alone to create Guoot. After a long time of creation Guoot came out of the house very well created and handsome.

The Mother ran and held him; "Guoot," called the Mother, "Who am I? Do you know me?"

Guoot said, "No," he did not know her.

"This is not my son Guoot. Why is he not knowing?" said the Mother.

The Lioness took Guoot back to the house of Creation. After long time in Creation Guoot came out, stood in front of the house, looked round and he instantly called his Mother.

"Exactly, this is my Guoot, the son of my friend, Mabeek," said the Mother.

The sister of Guoot came and said, 'Is this Guoot my brother?'

"Yes," said the Koor.

The sister of Guoot said that his brother used to beat a dog when running. So, a dog was set to run against Guoot. The dog out ran him.

"No, no, this is not our Guoot," she said.

The Lioness took Guoot back into house of creation.

After a long time in creation, Guoot came out and he was set to run against the dog. He beat the dog in running.

The sister of Guoot said, "Exactly, this is Guoot my brother."

When the people were about to leave, the girl Guoot had planned to marry, came and said, "Guoot, who was to be my husband, used to run faster than wind." Guoot was set to run against the wind. The wind surpassed him in running. The girlfriend said, "No, no, this is not Guoot my husband."

The Koor took Guoot back into the house of Creation. After a long time of creation, Guoot came out and was set to run against the wind, Guoot surpassed the wind in running. After this creation, everybody was satisfied about Guoot.

When the people were about to leave the Lioness's home, one youth threw a spear into the Lioness, slashing out her stomach. She fell dead. Her husband came out very furious.

"Why killed my wife? Has she not created your Guoot?"asked the Lion, trembling violently.

"She has created him, but why did she eat him in the first place?" asked one of the youths.

The husband of the dead Lioness suddenly leapt upon one youth, breaking his neck. One youth threw the spear on him, and he fell down dead. Another youth came running, holding up a spear. An old man saw him, and he quickly shouted at him to not spear the Lion again, but unfortunately, he threw the spear for the second time. Immediately, the Lion stood up, alive and very wild. Indeed, a serious taboo had been broken. According to the taboos, the Lion is not speared twice. The first spear takes life out of him, and the second spear brings the life back into him. Here, the second spear made Koor the Lion into Ajuong the Monster. Ajuong is fiercer than Koor the Lion. Ajuong is undying and does not feel pain. Ajuong ran to the people, breaking another man's neck.

Ajuong kept running amongst the people, killing one man after another. All the youth stood on their feet, doubling, tripling and quadrupling the spears upon the Ajuong and finally one youth grabbed him by the tail, swirling him down. They slit its throat.

After that the youth left for the cattle camp. Ajuong came back to life, and he ran ahead of the youth in the forest and hiding himself in the grass. When the youth arrived, the Ajuong came, dispersing himself into them like a swarm of bees, "What killed my wife? Has he not created your Guoot?"He attacked the youth, killing one youth after another. The youth stood their ground, with a strong heart, they doubled, tripled and quadrupled spears upon the Ajuong and finally youth grabbed him by tail, swirling him down. They slit its throat.

"The Ajuong fell as if it was dead but he will later come and waylay us. What can we do?" asked one youth.

"Let someone go and call the elders in the camp," said another youth.

The fastest runner was sent to the cattle camp. The elders came and told the youth to cut the Ajuong into pieces.

At that time, then, the Lion was cut into pieces and the pieces were scattered in grasses and trees.

And they left.

Later, after the people had gone, the Ajuong came back to life, ran ahead of them in the forest and hid himself in the grass. When the people arrived there, the Ajuong came out, furiously moving amongst the people like a swarm of bees. He roared, "What killed my wife? Did she not create your Guoot?" The Ajuong attacked the people, killing and breaking the neck of one after another. The people stood their ground, with a strong heart and doubling, tripling and quadrupling the spears upon the Ajuong and finally a man grabbed him by tail, swirling him down. They slit its throat.

One of the oldest men said since the Ajuong had been killed and it was bringing himself back to life and brining breathe into himself, he would keep on eating the people. He should be cut into pieces and burned into ashes and the ashes scattered into thickets.

The Ajuong was cut into pieces and was set on the fire. As the people were burning the Ajuong on the biggest fire, one claw of the Ajuong sparkled out of the fire, bouncing up and down, dashing into the grass.

After they scattered the ashes in to the grass and water, the people went to the cattle camp.

The Claw went and transformed itself into another monster called Riop e Koor / Riop de Ajuong the Claw of the Monster / Lion, the most fiercest of the previous two animals. He had a scaly skin, a skin as hard and slippery as the claw of the Lion. At midnight the Riop e Koor attacked the cattle camp, greedily eating the people, one after another. The people threw spears on him, but the spears were slipping off. The people continued, doubled, tripled and quadrupled the spears upon the Riop e Koor, but they kept slipping off its scaly body. Finally, people away ran away with their cows and children. And the Riop e Koor had to chase them; he was cruelly chasing them for many days. He ate so many people they could not be counted.

After the Riop scattered the cattle camp, and ate the people, the elders in the village had nothing to do but to invite a Magician. He came and he staged his divine powers, conjuring up the Riop. As a result of this, the Riop fell into a deep sleep. People went and found him, they pierced out his eyes while he was asleep in the spell. The Riop e Koor was then blind. In the forest he wandered and roamed until he died of hunger.

Gegen: The Most Gluttonous Man

O nce upon a time there was the most gluttonous man called Gegen. In those days, there was no food. His family was suffering from hunger. Aneet's leaves plucked by the wife was the food they ate. One evening, his wife did not bring the food so Gegen drank the milk and slept in his cattle byre. That became his habit, if the wife had not brought the food, he drank the milk alone, without giving any to the children or the wife.

One night the wife gave birth, so in the afternoon she didn't go to the forest to pluck leaves. In the evening the wife sent the children to Gegen at the cattle byre at the edge of the farm. She wanted the milk, he refused, chasing back the children.

That night, the wife went to the Lion's home and found them sleeping in the house. She opened the granary, stealing the sorghum and she returned to her home.

Before she could go home, she pounded the sorghum, cooked it in the house of the neighbor who lived very far away. She put the food of Gegen, her husband, in a big calabash and food for the children in another, and she came home. After she arrived home, she sent the children to call Gegen to come and eat.

"Wa, the mother said you must come to eat," said the children.

"Go back, I don't want to eat Aneet's leaves anymore," said he.

"Waa, it is not Aneet-leaf food. It is sorghum food," said the children.

"Go away, you think, you can trick me so you can drink my milk today?" he said while laughing. "Where did you get the sorghum? Why didn't I hear the sound of the pestle in the mortar, pounding it?"

The children returned home.

The Mother put a small amount of food in the hands of each child, and she sent them back to Gegen in the cattle byre. When he saw the food, Gegen grabbed it

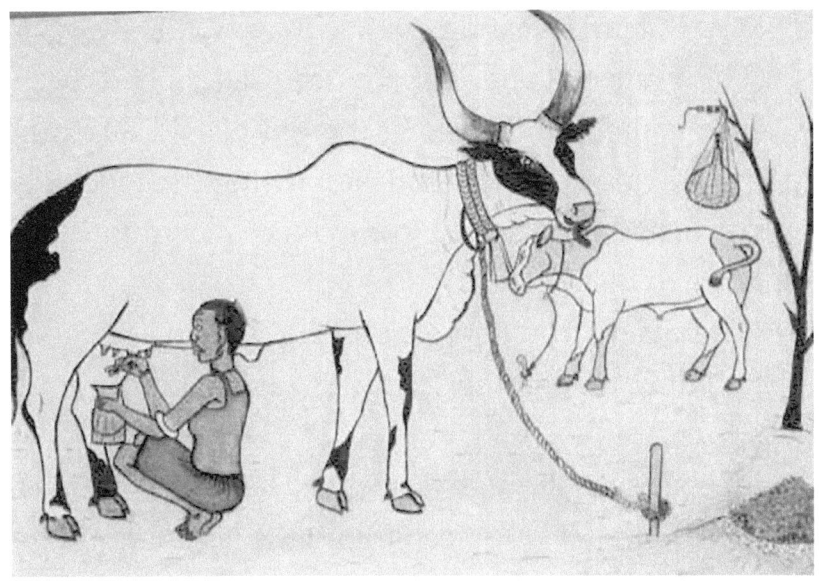

out of the children's hands, swallowing it and he came running home. As he dashed out quickly from the cattle byre, the cow knocked out one of his eyes but he did not feel it.

The wife gave him the food. With the spoon he scooped the food and he was throwing it into his mouth while asking:

"Where have you ….?" before he could finish the question, he threw the food into his mouth.

"Waa, your eye is bleeding," said of one of the children.

"Sweat," he replied to his children.

"Untrue. It is blood, not sweat," said one of the children.

"Stop it, I am sweating."

With gluttony and impatience Gegen had been eating the food while asking the unfinished question to his wife. After he had finished eating the food and was satisfied, he finally completed his unfinished sentence to his wife.

"Where have you got this food?"

"I got it in that anthill," his wife said, pointing at an anthill.

Gegen rushed, brought a hoe, and he started digging up the anthill. He dug deeper into the anthill until the hole reached his waist. As he was digging, with sweat dribbling like a rain over him, his wife came over to the hole, carrying some sorghum in her hands. To mock him she threw some sorghum into the hole and she said:

"Look, there is the sorghum. You have almost reached it." When Gegen saw the sorghum was nearer he increased his power, he intensified the digging. His wife threw some sorghum again.

"Look they are near," shouted the wife. Gegen kept on digging the hole deeper and deeper and there was no sorghum. Thus, his wife told him to stop to rest and that he should resume in the evening.

After a short rest, he started digging again but there was sorghum coming forth. His wife finally told him she had lied to him, and that she would show him later at night where she got the grains.

Gegen waited impatiently as if the night would not fall.

"When will the night come now, so that my wife shows me where she gets the sorghum?" Gegen complained to himself.

As soon as the sun set, Gegen told his wife to show him the place. His wife said he should sleep first and she would wake him up. So Gegen went to sleep. At midnight, the wife woke him up. They left for Lion's home to steal the sorghum. The wife was leading the way and Gegen was following her secretly and earnestly until they reached the Lions' home. They found the Lions were deeply sleeping in the house, their tails crept and coiling like pumpkin stems. The wife took a two-headed pole and pushed up the cover of the granary, opening it. Gegen and his wife climbed into granary. The wife filled the basket with grains while Gegen ate uncooked and dry sorghum. He was chewing it noisily, with a rolling sound as though he were a grinding stone.

His wife whispered to him, "Gegen chew the grains slowly because your sound will wake up the Lions."

He refused.

His wife whispered again, "Gegen let us leave, the

day is about to break and the Lions will wake up."

"Let me fill my mouth with grains so that I can chew them on the way," he said.

His wife said, "You take them quickly."

Gegen had filled his mouth full of grains and they climbed down from the granary. When Gegen was climbing down, he was chewing the sorghum, when he reached the ground he swallowed the grains and his mouth was empty. Gegen turned and he climbed up the granary. His wife asked, "Where are you going again, Gegen?"

"I am going to fill my mouth and hands with sorghum so that I can eat them on the way," he answered.

"Take them quickly," said his wife.

Gegen filled the sorghum in his mouth and hands, and he climbed down from granary, and they left. When they reached the Lion's farm, Gegen had already finished the sorghum in his mouth and hands, and he told his wife that he wanted return to the granary. His wife refused, persuading Gegen not to go back to the granary because the day was almost breaking. Gegen did not listen and he went back to the granary. So the wife left him and she went home alone.

Gegen climbed up the granary, and he was chewing the sorghum until the day broke. When the Lions woke up, they heard the sound of something chewing sorghum in the granary.

"What is in the granary? Is it a rat?" the Lion's wife asked herself. She checked the granary, she found the human being in the granary.

"Who are you?" asked the Lion's wife.

"I am Gegen."

"You are the one, who has always been eating, finishing our grains, come out, thief," said the Lion's wife.

Gegen came out; his shrank, disappeared into his stomach and became his kidneys. All the Lions came, surrounding him.

One Lion said, "He will be our food today, we shall not go to hunt for meat again. One good day is better than one month."

Gegen allowed himself the wind, crying loud and bitterly, begging the Lions not to kill him and that he had a wife and children who he could bring to the Lions. The Lions changed their minds and agreed to what Gegen was asking them to do. They sent Gegen with two Lions, to go bring his family.

When the wife saw Gegen approaching with two Lions, she ran with her children but the two ran speedily on both sides and encircled them.

When the wife refused to go the Lions' home, Gegen assured her that he had made an agreement with the Lions that they should not eat, him and his family. The Lions escorted Gegen to their home.

They slept in the Lion's home. In the morning, before the Lions would go to hunt, the Father Lion said, "Gegen we are going to hunt, you let your wife kill one of your children and cook it for us as our food in the evening and let her cook sorghum for yourself and your family."

"It is good, I will myself kill the child and she will cook it," Gegen told the Lions.

The Lions used to go together for hunting with their cubs and Gegen and his family remained at home.

Immediately, after the Lions had left, Gegen asked his wife, "Which child will we cook for the Lions as their food in the evening?"

"Are you mad?" said the wife, "There is no child to be cooked as Lions' food in evening."

"Then, what will the Lions eat in the evening?" he asked.

"Stop talking, I know what to do," said the wife, "I will cook for them the frogs."

"What if the Lion discover that it is a frog? Will they not stop giving sorghum?" asked Gegen.

"They will not discover because I will shave the hairs of the child and put hairs in the frogs and I will hide the child in the hollow in the big tamarind tree on the farm."

"What if the Lions asks for the bones and head of the child?"

"I will tell them that I threw the head and bones away because we are relatives and relatives do not eat bones and head of another relative, it kills people because the relationship is in the bone."

Then the wife went to the pond and collected frogs, bringing them home. She shaved one child's head and she cooked the hair with frogs in the pot. And she hid the child in the hollow of the tamarind tree on the farm.

In the evening, the Lions came. Gegen gave them the meat in pot.

"This is the meat of one of my children,"he said.

The Lions ate. When they were eating, one old Lion asked,

"Geg-Genn (Gegen is pronounced as Geg-Genn in Lionic, a language spoken by Lions), where are the bones and head of this child?"

"My wife had thrown them away, said Geg-Genn, "Because we are relatives with you. And the relationship is inside the bone and that is why the Hyena does not eat the head of human beings, to avoid death."

"Really, this is why it is said a big person doesn't know other things. I am big but I know not. A human kept learning until aging. I don't know these things but I learn it now," said the old Lion.

In the morning, the Father-Lion said, "Geg-Genn, we are going to hunt, let your wife cook sorghum for yourself and your family but let her kill one of your children and cook it for our food for the evening."

Then all the Lions left for the hunting. Geg-Genn's wife went to the pond, brought the frogs, shaved another child's head, cooked frogs in a pot, added the hairs and then hid the child in a big hollow of the tamarind tree on farm.

The Lions came and ate the meat in the evening.

After six days the Father-Lion said, "Geg-Genn, we are going to hunt, let your wife cook sorghum for yourself and your family but let her kill one of your children and cook it as our food for the evening."

"My children are finished," said Geg-Genn.

"Then, you cook your wife," said the Father Lion.

Geg-Genn agreed.

After the Lions had left for hunting, Geg-Genn's wife went to the pond, she brought the frogs. Geg-Genn shaved her head and she cooked the frogs and her hair in the pot. She also cooked the food for her family. They ate. When it was a time for Lions to come, Geg-Genn's wife climbed into the hollow in the tamarind tree. The Lions came and ate the meat.

In the following morning, the Lion-Father said, "Geg-Genn you kill yourself and cook yourself to be our food in the evening."

Geg-Genn agreed.

After the Lion left for hunting, the wife of Geg-Genn climbed down, she shaved Geg-Genn's head, brought frogs from the pond, she cooked them with his hair in the pot. She also cooked the food for her children. They ate. When the time came for the Lion to come, she and Geg-Genn climbed into the hollow.

The Lion came, they ate Geg-Genn "Geg-Genn has cooked himself well," one of the Lion said as they were eating him.

On the morning, after they ate Geg-Genn, the Lions left for hunting. The Lions got the giraffe and they chased him, driving him until they came and pulled him down, killing him under the tamarind where Geg-Genn and his family were hiding in the hollow. The Lions started to burn the giraffe's meat under the tamarind while Geg-Genn was looking down at them. When the Lions were busy eating the meat, Geg-Genn's heart melted and his mouth began dripping with water because of the fatty meat being eaten by the Lions below.

Geg-Genn lost his patience, and began saying in low voices, "My mouth, my mouth, my mouth," he breathed deep, and was slobbering like a baby. His wife also said in a low voice, "Geg-Genn, Geg-Genn, you will let children be eaten by the Lions."

Geg-Genn looked side to side. Suddenly, heart

fallen and crying loudly, "My mouth, my mouth , my mouth." The Lions heard the voice and were surprised who was crying.

"Who are you?"

"I am Geg-Genn."

"Geg-Genn, are you not dead?" the Lions asked.

"No, I am here with my family," Geg-Genn said.

"Come down with your family," said the Lion Father. He came down.

"Why did you deceive us, Geg-Genn?"

"I am sorry. Forgive me. I will do whatever you tell me but now let me eat meat with you."

Geg-Genn ate the meat with them. They slept.

In the morning, the Lions said, "Geg-Genn, cook one of your children as our food for the evening."

"Okay," Geg-Genn said.

The Lions left for hunting. His wife told Geg-Genn that they had to leave the Lions' home.

Geg-Genn refused and he said, "Where shall we go and get food?"

His wife left with the children and Geg-Genn remained in the Lions' home. In the evening, when the Lions came they found that there was no child cooked for them, and there were no children, because the children had escaped with their Mother. It was only Geg-Genn and they could not go to sleep without eating anything. So they broke the neck of Geg-Genn, eating him as their food for the evening.

Chapter 3

Achol: The Most Emancipated Daughter

O nce upon a time there was a daughter of a rich and great chief. Her name was Achol. She was such a beautiful girl; she wasn't bathing with water. She was first washed with churned milk and rinsed with the fresh milk. She wasn't working. She had not been doing anything from childhood until she became an adult. She had been staying in the cattle camp all her life until she got married. She was not eating food of sorghum, she only ate the cream of milk. When she wanted to eat the food of sorghum, sometime her food was not cooked by water but with butter. When the cattle camps travelled from one place to another, she was not carrying anything in her hands. When she saw people carrying pegs, ropes and gourds on their heads, she would also imitate them by carrying her own hands on her head. When someone who had been carrying heavy luggage, and cried of neck pain, she would also imitate them, crying that her own hands were the heaviest and she had a pain in her neck.

When she became an adult, a man called Thabiya married her. When she was given to Thabiya, her Father said that the home of his daughter should be built near his home, so that his daughter should be helped by her Mother. Thaibya came and built his house near his Father-in-law's home.

When the time for Achol as a guest finished, Thabiya told her to start to work and he said:

"Achol, sweep the floor."

Achol refused to sweep the floor of the home and she called out, "Mama, Mama...."

"Yes, my daughter," answered her Mother.

"Thabiya says, I should sweep the floor of the home yard."

Her Mother came and she swept the floor, and she returned to her home. That was early morning.

"Achol, milk the cows," said Thabiya.

Achol refused to milk the cows and she called;

"Mama, Mama...."

"Yes, my daughter,"answered her Mother.

"Thabiya says, I milk the cows"

Her Mother came and said, "please Thabiya my son, don't disturb Achol, she is your sister, and she is a child." She milked the cows and she returned to her home. That was late morning.

Thabiya said, "Achol go and bring water from the pond."

"Mama, Mama," Achol called out

"Yes, my daughter," answered her Mother,

"Thabiya said, I should go to bring water from the pond."

Her Mother came and said, "Please Thabiya, my son, don't disturb Achol, she is your sister and she is a child." She went to the pond and she brought the water.

And she returned to her Mother. That was now the afternoon.

Thabiya said, "Achol, take sorghum and pound it in mortar."

"Mama Mama…," Achol called out.

"Yes, my daughter," answered her Mother.

"Thabiya said, I pound sorghum in mortar."

Her Mother came and said, "Please Thabiya my son, don't disturb Achol, she is your sister and she is a child.' Her Mother took sorghum and she pounded them and she cooked their food and she gave Achol her food and Thabiya his food and she returned to her home.

In this way Achol had been refusing to work and she had been calling her Mother to come to work for her every day. Thabiya got tired, and he went to the Lion who was aman-eater. He told him, "Please Lion the man-eater, can you come and eat for me my Mother-in-law."

"Why?" asked the man-eater.

She doesn't allow my wife to work.

"Where is she?" asked Lion the man-eater.

"Her house is near my home," said Thabiya.

Thabiya came and he shown his Mother-in-law's house during the day. At night Lion the man-eater came and ate Achol's Mother. The Lion removed one of Achol's Mother's legs and he locked the door with it.

In the following morning, Thabiya said, "Achol sweep the floor." Achol refused as usual and she called:

"Mama, Mama, Mama, Mama...." Her Mother didn't answer her call. She called again "Mama, Mama, Mama." Her Mother never answered her call. So Achol went to her Mother's house, she saw her Mother's leg barred the closure mat of the door. She opened the house and she saw the blood on the floor. Achol cried bitterly and she returned to her home. And there was no one to work for her. So, Achol started to sweep the floor, milk the cow and bring the water from the pond. She took sorghum to the mortar when she pounded them, her hands were bleeding on the pestle, when she pounded again her hands bled on the pestle. Achol cried and bled on the mortar.

ALAL: The Most Beautiful Girl

O nce upon a time, there lived the most beautiful girl called Alal. Alal was glorified and adored her by Father with everything good on earth. The Father bought her a personality ox and, in the culture, it is only a boy who owns a pet bull. He bought her a bell and, in the culture, it is only a boy who owns a bell. She adopted a pet dog. Her dog was the biggest dog in the whole cattle camp. Alal had a cousin called Juec.

Because of her beauty Juec, her cousin, melted like a gum in the dry season. He said he wanted to marry her as his wife. Alal bitterly rejected him but Juec cruelly insisted that he had to marry her or else he would kill himself. Alal was running mad, imagining herself in the same papyrus mat with Juec as a husband and wife. The Father of Alal and father of Juec were from the same Mother and Father.

When Juec's love for Alal became a big problem in the cattle camp, they were sent home to their parents. At home, both Fathers also rejected the marriage condemning it straightway. The parents said Alal and Juec could not marry each other because they have a close blood relationship and if indeed they did marry many people in their families would die of illness because of

incest. Juec swore that if he could not marry Alal, he would kill himself.

So, elders in the community met and discussed the marriage, they agreed instead of Juec killing himself, he should be allowed to marry Alal. And the blood relationship would be cut in the ceremony like what is usually done if relatives have sexual intercourse with each other by mistake. The elders said a goat should be taken to the forest and cut into two.

When Juec heard that the elders had approved his marriage to Alal, he celebrated the decision and said, "instead of cutting the goat into two to cut the relation, it is my personality ox (Majok) that should be cut into two."

Juec married Alal with fifty head of cattle. His black and white pet bull was taken to the forest and slaughtered as a sacrifice to cut the blood relationship. The bull was cut into two, and this ended the families' blood relation. To expiate the bone relationship, the thigh-bone of bull was brought out. And then Juec and Alal were to hold the bone, each at one end, holding it with both hands and their eldest uncle beat the bone in the middle and the bone broke into many pieces. The bone crushed and did not break evenly into two.

After the bone was broken to separate their tie as brother and sister and unite them as husband and wife, the Mother of Alal did not shout the shrill to marriage and neither did all the other women.

"As this one bone had broken into two, it is a sign that the blood relationship of Juec and Alal is also cut and therefore Juec and Alal are not relatives anymore but different people and they have married each other today," declared the their uncle.

"Women, why don't you shout the shrill to the marriage?" called one of the elders.

"There is a problem, why hasn't the bone broken evenly in the middle?" asked the Mother of Alal.

Alal was taken to Juec's family home. Before the sun set, Alal acquired herself the sharpest knife and hid under the papyrus. At night Alal lovingly talked to Juec before sleeping. At last, when they were about to sleep as a husband and a wife, Alal cut off the genitals of Juec using the sharpest knife, and she ran out of the house. Juec died.

Alal went back to her Father's home. At her Father's home that night, Alal took both her dog and bell. Alal went to the house where the girls were sleeping and she rang the bell near house. The girls heard the sound, and they came out:

"What is that sound like the bell of Alal?" asked the girls.

"It is me, my sisters," Alal said.

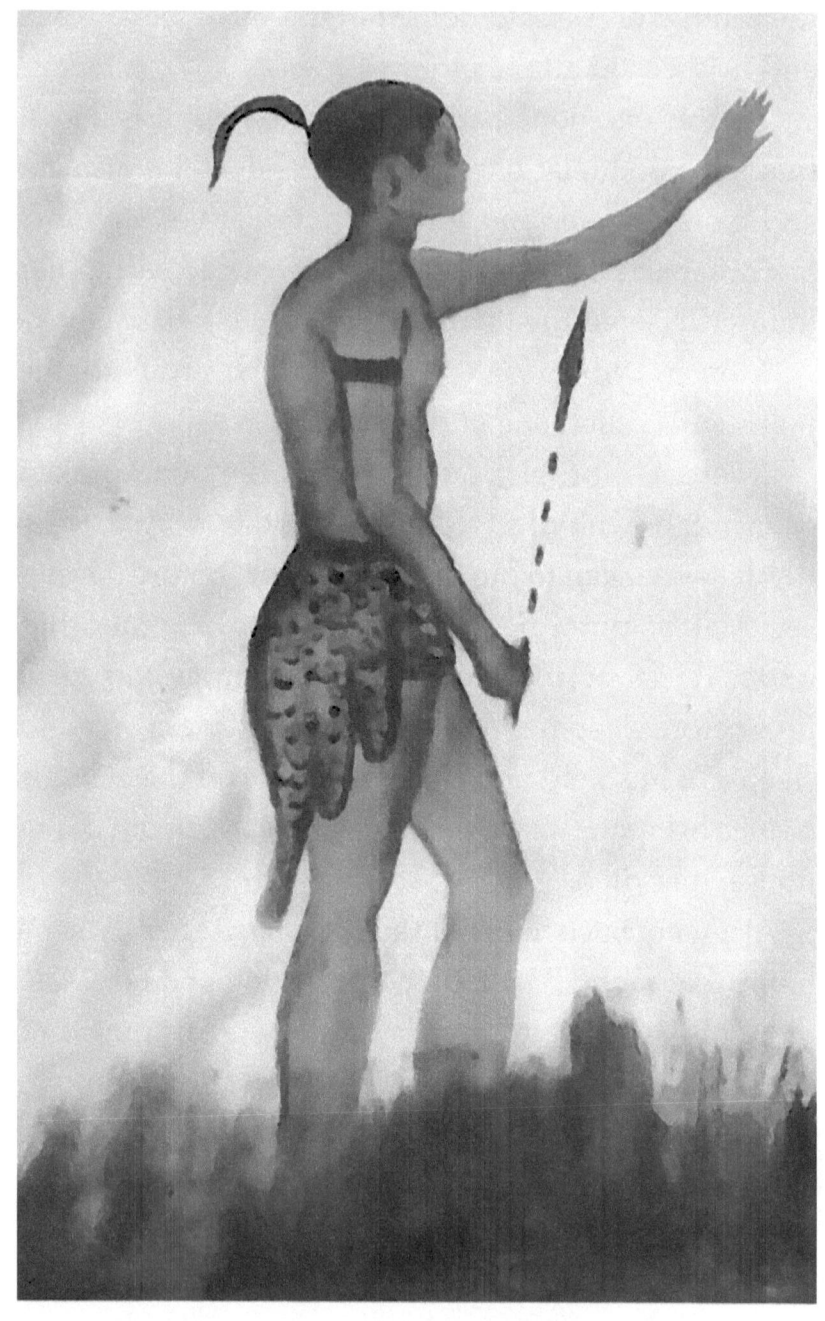

"Why do you ring the bell at midnight?" the girls asked.

"It is bad luck that has befallen me in my generation. It has come to its end tonight. I cut the umblical cord of my cousin, Juec," Alal said.

"You did the right thing, our sister," the girls said.

"What are you doing now?" the girls asked.

"I am going to stay in the forest alone because I became the only unlucky one of my generation on this earth," Alal said.

"Our sister we shall go with you because, if we remain it will also be our turn to be married to our cousin like you," said the girls.

All the girls in that village left and followed Alal.

Alal was now travelling with her dog and the other girls. Alal arrived in another village and she rang the bell near the house, where the girls were sleeping, the girls heard the bell and woke up.

"What is that sounds like the bell of Alal?" asked the girls.

"It is me, my sisters," Alal said.

"Why do you ring the bell at midnight?" the girls asked.

"Because this marriage, that was bad luck, is over," Alal said.

"You did the right thing, our sister," the girls asked

"Where are you going now?" the girls asked.

"I am going into the forest," Alal said.

""Our sister we shall go with you," the girls said.

Throughout the night Alal gathered hundreds of girls from different villages and she immigrated with them into the forest.

In the forest Alal, together with the girls, entered an anthill. Everyday in the evening, when the sun was setting, the girls would come out, and they woman-danced (dany).[3]

After some days passed, a cattle camp came and pegged in the nearby forest. One day the boys came near the anthill, they found the girls dancing at sunset. The boys ran to the cattle camp to tell people that there were a group of many girls dancing in the forest. They were rebuked for telling lies. The boys stopped talking about the girls. Another day the boys came and sat on the anthill. One of the girls pierced one boy's buttock with needle. The boy bled and he ran to the cattle camp. He showed it to the people, what the girls had done to him. When the people saw the boy bleeding, they accepted that the girls existed. On the next day, young men came and sat on anthill, the girls pierced another man's buttock. The people returned and believed that the girls existed in the anthill.

After that, all the young men were told to go to take

these girls as their wives. In the afternoon, the men came and hid themselves in grass near the anthill. When the girls came out to dance before the sun set, the men ran to them, scrambling the girls, and taking them a wives. During the grabbing of the girls by the men, Alal entered into her dog. After all the girls were taken, some men missed out. They had not got girls, because, the number of men was greater than the number of girls. Alal's cousin told one of the men who missed out on a girl, to take the dog. The man refused. Ajak, the son of the chief of that clan had also missed out. Alal's cousin went to him, and she told him to take the dog.

"What am I going to do with a dog?" asked Ajak.

"It can guard your goats and sheep, you cannot leave something living behind, it can curse you," said the cousin of Alal.

Finally, Ajak accepted and he took the dog. Everyone who got a girl went home happy. When Ajak arrived with the dog, his Mother was angered by the dog, and she asked: "Why do you bring the dog home while your age-mates are bringing beautiful girls as wives? When I always insult you as a weak, useless child, you get angry and you say I insult you for nothing. Haven't you proven what I have always been saying now? Ajak my son, I wish, I would not have a child than to have you at all." When Ajak saw his Mother was annoyed, blaming him, he left the dog at home and went to the cattle camp.

In evening, the cousin of Alal went to Ajak's Mother, and she told her to treat the dog well. She said the dog should not be given food in a shard of a pot but in the decorated calabash of a guest.

"Go away," jeered Ajak's Mother, "In which village is a dog given food in calabashes of the guest? Is the dog a guest?"

When the Mother of Ajak was angered, the cousin of Alal left. The Mother of Ajak gave food to the dog in a broken piece of pot in the house of the sheep and goats. After she left, Alal came out of the dog, and she ate the food, and she went back into the dog.

At dawn everyday, Alal was coming out of the dog, and she swept the floor of Ajak's Mother's home as well as the neighbour's home. When the people woke up in the morning, they found the floors were clean.

"Who sweeps our floor?" they asked themselves and none of the people knew who swept their floors.

One afternoon, the Mother of Ajak gave the food to the dog in the goat and sheep house. Alal came out of the dog and she was eating. The small grandson looked through the window, he saw Alal, and he ran to his grandMother.

"GrandMother there is a girl eating in the house of the goat and sheep." The grandMother entered the house. When Alal saw her, she ran, but the Mother caught her, and held her by both hands.

Alal changed herself into snake, but the Mother still held her tightly. Alal changed herself into scorpion, but the Mother still held her tightly. Alal changed herself into many dangerous animals but Ajak's Mother had not stopped holding her tightly.

"Mother, have you tested me? Have you hardened your heart for me?" asked Alal.

"Yes I tested and hardened my heart for you," answered the Mother.

"Leave me, I will not run away," said Alal and she stopped.

Ajak's Mother, who had just become the Mother-in-law of Alal, hurriedly sent someone to Ajak in the cattle camp, to bring the milk in a big gourd of a guest. The messenger went to cattle camp and told Ajak what his Mother said.

"Why is my Mother requesting milk in a gourd of a guest?" Ajak asked the messenger, "who has become a guest at home?"

"I don't know," said the messenger.

Ajak milked the milk and he took it to his Mother in the small gourd of the boys.

"Why do you bring the milk in the small gourd of boys? I sent you the message to bring in a big gourd of a guest" asked the Mother.

"Who is a guest here?" asked Ajak.

"Roll up that papyrus," said the Mother.

Alal was covered up, down under three papyrus mats. Ajak rolled the first papyrus mat, threw it away and asked his mother:

"Where is it?"

"You rolled up the other mats," said the Mother.

Ajak rolled out the second and the third mats, and he immediately found an extremely beautiful Alal. When Alal saw Ajak, she ran but Ajak caught her. Alal changed herself into a snake but Ajak held her tightly. Alal changed herself into scorpion but still Ajak held her tightly.

"Have you tested and hardened your heart for me," asked Alal.

"Yes, I tested and hardened my heart for you," Ajak answered.

"Leave me, I will not run away," said Leek-Leek.

Ajak gently sat her down, then quickly ran back to the cattle camp, milking the milk into the big gourd of a guest, and returning home as fast as possible. Ajak was very, very happy for his beautiful bride Alal, who was a dog when the men grabbed the girls at the anthill.

FOLKTALES FROM SOUTH SUDAN

Ajak took Alal to the cattle camp, where she became the most beautiful wife in the whole cattle camp. All the people in the cattle camp, wished they knew they should have taken the dog that day on the anthill.

All the young men were now looking at Alal with exciting passion, desiring her. One day Ajak, together with the young men went to forest to tend the cows, the young men killed Ajak in the forest and left for the cattle camp.

The Dog of Alal, who was a Creator, breathed the life back into Ajak. Ajak woke up from the death and he followed the men to the camp. The men saw Ajak they were shocked.

"What happened? Have we not killed him before? Why is he still alive?" they asked themselves in secret.

Ajak didn't tell Alal what happened to him in the forest and neither did the Dog.

Some days passed. Ajak and the same men went again to tend the cows in the forest and they killed Ajak, cutting him into pieces and scattering his body in the forest. Then they left for the cattle camp. The Dog collected Ajak and breathed life back to him. And Ajak and Dog followed them to the cattle camp.

This time, the Dog went straight to Alal, told her what had been happening to Ajak her husband, he was killed two times, and he, the Dog had breathed the life back into him.

Alal sent the Dog to bring the Medicine of Death. At night, Alal mixed the medicine into ashes and she poured ashes around the cattle camp. All young men, who were of the same age as Ajak, died that night. In the morning, there was a great mourning. The Fathers, Mothers and wives of the dead men, were upset of what had happened. Ajak was the only young man who was alive.

When people were about to bury the young dead men, one of the elders said, they should not bury them before they knew the cause of the death. A Magician was called in to divine what was the cause.

A bull was slaughtered. The Magician looked into stomach of the bull. The Magician said that it was Alal who poured down the Ashes of Death. The whole cattle camp came and bowed before Alal, begging her to wake up the young men from death.

"Is death good?" Alal asked the whole cattle camp.

"No, death is the worst thing," said the people

"Why have the young men been killing my husband in the forest?" asked Alal.

The people felt sorry and apologized to Alal. Alal agreed and she poured down the flour of life at the edge of cattle camp, and all the young men woke up from death.

Leek-Leek:
The Beloved Husband

Once upon a time there was a man called Leek-Leek, who lived with his wife called Acany. Acany used to go dance, going every day, and Leek-Leek, her husband remained at home. Leek-Leek had been allowing Acany to go as an honour to the glory of loving her. Whenever Acany returned from the dance at night, she was always calling out her husband, from far:

"Leek-Leek, Leek-Leek my husband, open the door for me."

"Who are you?" he asked.

"I am Acany, your wife," she answered.

"Where are you coming from Acany? he asked.

"I am coming from the dance," she said.

"Acany who danced with you?" he asked.

"Raven danced with me," she said.

"Which Raven?" he asked.

"Raven the black the handsome! Who wears twilight strings of beads (made of ostrich egg shell) who used to dance with Leek-Leek! Who is as handsome and tall as Leek-Leek my husband," she explained.

"Good Acany, my wife," said he, "so open the door, enter the house, you have reached your home."

From far, where Acany was calling, Acany came near to the door.

"Acany if you are the wife of my Father's cows," her husband said, "You open the door slowly and quietly."

Acany opened the door slowly, and she entered quietly into the house.

"Acany if you are the wife of my Father's cows," said he, "you bring my food and put it down respectfully and gloriously before me."

Acany brought the food and put it down respectfully. Leek-Leek ate, then Acany came, and took away the calabash.

"Acany, if you are the wife of my Father's cows, you come."

For many years, Acany had been going to dance,

whenever she came back, she called out from afar for Leek-Leek and they talked lovingly. One day, after Acany had already left for the dance, her Mother followed her to the dance. Before the dance finished, the Mother of Acany left and returned home early. From afar, she called out:

"Lek-Lek, Lek-Lek, my husband, opens for me the door."

"Who are you?" he asked.

"I am Acieny, your wife," she said.

"Who danced with you?" he asked.

"The Crow danced with me," she said.

"Which Crow?" he asked.

"Crow, who is handsome like Lek-Lek, who used to dance with Lek-Lek a long time ago, who wears a twilight string of beads, who is tall like Lek-Lek," she said.

"Acany, the wife of my Father's cows, open the door, you have reached your home," he said.

Acieny came near to the door.

"Acany, if you are the wife of my Father's cows, open the door slowly."

Acieny pulled the mat-enclosure of the door, and threw it away roughly, and she entered the house with a lot of noise.

"Acany, if you are the wife of my Father's cows, you bring my food and put it down respectfully and gloriously," he said.

Acieny brought the food and she put it down noisily. Leek-Leek ate; Acieny came and carried away the calabash.

"Acany, if you are the wife of Father's cows, you come," said he.

Acieny came and threw herself down. Leek-Leek went out, picked some dry grass, he lit the fire and he came to look at Acany by the firelight, he found, it was not Acany his wife but her Mother, his Mother-in-law who tricked him, pretending like Acany. "I knew," Leek-Leek said, "My lovely wife Acany never pronounced me "Lek-Lek" or herself "Acieny." Leek-Leek put down the fire; he picked up his spears, and left his home at midnight. He moved into the forest, going where he did not know.

After Leek-Leek left, Acany arrived in farm, and she called out as usual.

"Leek-Leek, Leek-Leek my husband, open for me the door." Nobody answered her. Acany called out again, but nobody answered her. She came, entered the house, she did not find Leek-Lfeek.

"Where is Leek-Leek my husband?" she asked her Mother.

"I don't know," her Mother said.

"Why you don't know? Were you not here at home?" asked Acany.

"I just saw him with his spear and he went on that path," the Mother said.

Acany came out, and she ran after him. She didn't reach him. Acany found people on the path. "People, has the husband of mine, passed here?"

"What is your husband wearing?" asked the people

"He is wearing two rings of elephant tusk on his two arms. Ostrich feathers on his head and a string of the whitest beads on his neck."

"What is the problem with your husband?"

"It is my Mother who disgusted him," said Acany.

"Acany is your Mother still with her old things? You go this path, we saw your husband following it but he is very far," the people said.

Acany ran faster and faster. She found a group of giraffes grazing, "Group of Giraffes, have you seen my husband passing here?"

"What is he wearing?" asked the Giraffes.

"He is wearing two rings on his two arms, feathers on his head and the whitest beads on his neck," she said.

"What is the problem with your husband?" asked giraffes.

"It is my Mother who disgusted him," Acany said.

"Acany, is your Mother still with her old things? You go this path, we saw him following it, but he is far," said the Giraffes.

Acany ran faster and faster and she didn't reach Leek-Leek until daylight broke and she continued running all day until the sun set, so she slept on the path. In the morning, she took off, running until she reached the home of a female Elephant. Acany found the children of Elephant alone at home. The rain was about to pour. Acany took the sorghum of the Elephant from the floor into the granary. Acany also pounded the sorghum of the Elephant into flour and she put it in the basket. After that Acany went and hid herself in the cattle byre of the Elephant. When the Elephants saw rain coming, she ran home but she was washed on the way by the rain before she could reach home. The Elephant said to herself, "my sorghum has been washed away by the rain now." When she arrived home, she found her sorghum was taken inside the granary, she was surprised, she asked her children, "who took the sorghum in the granary?" Her children answered that they were the ones.

Afterwards the Elephant's children told their Mother that, "there is a human being who took sorghum inside granary."

"Where is that human being?" asked the Elephant.

"She is hiding in the byre," said the children.

The Elephant went and found Acany in the byre, she congratulated her so much and she asked her what she wanted. Acany told her that her husband had run away from home, and she was following him. Acany said she was also very tired and she couldn't run anymore.

The Elephant said, "Do not worry Acany, I will carry you tomorrow on my back until we shall reach your husband."

Acany slept at the Elephant's home. In the morning the Elephant put Acany on her back and she ran very fast with her. In the afternoon, Acany told the Elephant that she had seen the head of Leek-Leek very far.

"So, Acany, can I put you down here since you have seen the head of your husband?" asked the Elephant.

"Yes," said Acany.

The Elephant put Acany down from her back and she returned to her home.

Acany ran for a short time and she reached Leek-Leek. When Leek-Leek saw Acany, he ran away. Acany chased Leek-Leek and she caught him. Leek-Leek was very, very angry, so he changed himself into a scorpion but Acany did not throw him away. He changed himself into a snake, but still Acany kept him. When Leek-Leek saw Acany, she held onto him strongly, he asked:

"Have you tested your heart for me, Acany?"

"Yes, I tested all my heart for you, my husband Leek-Leek," said Acany.

"Leave me, I will not run away," said Leek-Leek.

Leek-Leek agreed to return to his children and home. They set off on a journey back home. When they were walking in the forest, Leek-Leek got thirsty. Thus, he sent Acany to draw him the water in the river. When Acany was fetching the water, she fell into the river and the waves pulled her down under the water and she never appeared. When Leek-Leek saw Acany his wife taken by the river, his heart broke immediately, he hit his stomach with the spear, and he fell backward, dead. The waves carried away Acany under the water, and by luck, she went and swam out of the river at a far shore. When she returned, she found husband

had already killed himself with the spear. Acany cried bitterly, and deeply mourned her husband.

She went and she called all birds and animals who ate meat to come and eat Leek-Leek. Before they ate him she told them, "Please animals and birds, eat the flesh of Leek-Leek but do not touch one of his bones."

After the body of Leek-Leek was eaten, Acany came and collected all his bones. She counted them all and found that the blade-bone of the knee was missing.

"Animals and birds, the blade-knee bone of my husband is missing," said Acany.

The Lion who was leading the eating of flesh, called all birds and animals to vomit what they had eaten. All birds and animals vomited the flesh they had eaten. The vomit was checked and there was no bone in it.

The Vulture (Chuoor) refused to vomit the flesh he ate to be checked.

"I do not vomit, whatever I have eaten," said the Vulture.

"Why don't you vomit?" asked the Lion

"I am created like that."

The Lion got angry and he slapped the back of the Vulture. The Vulture vomited the flesh he had eaten. When it was checked, a blade-bone of the knee joint was found in it.

"Why did you call me if you did not want me to

swallow some bones," Vulture protested angrily.

Acany took all bones of Leek-Leek to the Creator. When Acany arrived at the Creator's home, she did not go straight home. She sat in the farm of the Creator, quietly and miserably. The Creator saw Acany, the Creator sent the Crow to call her home. The Crow went to Acany, "Woman, the Creator says bring you home," the Crow called Acany in an abusive language.

When Acany heard this, she refused to go with the Crow, so the Crow returned and Acany remained on the farm.

When the Creator saw Acany was not coming, Creator sent the Rat to call her home. The Rat came and said, "You wicked woman, the Creator needs you."

Acany refused to go to the Creator's home with the Rat.

When the Creator saw that Acany was not coming, the Creator sent the Weaver bird. The Weaver Bird came and said:

"Guest come; the Creator needs you."

Acany agreed and she came to the Creator's home with the Weaver Bird.

Acany told the Creator, what had happened to her husband. The Creator took the bones and gave them to the Crow to grind them into flour. The Crow ground the bones and before she could take the flour to Achiek the Creator , she scooped the flour by spoonfuls (thial) and the Crow ate it. The Creator was molding the new bones from flour, the flour was not enough to mold all the bones because of the missing spoonfuls of the flour.

The Crow was called, and she admitted she had eaten spoonfuls of flour. The Crow was forced to vomit back the flour. The Crow turned the flour back into bones. And the Creator gave the bones to the Weaver Bird, who honestly ground them into pure and full flour. When the Weaver Bird finished the grinding of the bone, she gave the powder to the Creator.

Then the Creator called Acany and asked her what her husband looked like. Acany said her husband looked like Raven the Black. The Creator told Acany to bring the Raven. Acany ran and called the Raven and brought him. The Creator created Leek-Leek exactly like the Raven.

After that the Creator gave Acany her handsome Leek-Leek. Acany fell down before the Creator; she worshipped and thanked the Creator.

When they were returning home, Acany killed the Viper snake on the way and she filled it's poison in a snail shell. Looking at the poison, Acany said she would see with this poison why her Mother corrupted her name Acany to Acieny and my husband's name

Leek-Leek to Lek-Lek that night.

On the day they arrived, Acany cooked the food and she put the snake's poison in the food of her Mother. Before she gave the food to her Mother she called her children in the house and she told them, "Today if your grandMother calls you and she gives the food on to your hands, you refuse and tell her, 'O, our grand-Mother you eat your food, you have been so hungry, when your daughter was not around.' "

And Acany took the food, and she gave it to her Mother. When the grandMother called her grand-children as usual to put the food on their hands, the grandchildren refused. The Mother of Acany ate the food alone and she died of snake poison.

Glossary - Pronunciation

Achiek (Aciëk), creator, someone born with bodily deformity

Achol:
The Last Born

Once there was a servant called Keny who reared and looked after the cows of a rich man. One day the cattle camp was moving from old pasture to the new, Keny had been driving the cows while carrying the little daughter of the rich man called Achol on his neck. Achol was very fat, young and she could not walk at all. On the way Achol became so heavy for Keny to carry and drive the cows at the same time. Thus, Keny put Achol down in the forest and he left her.

When Keny was asked about Achol in camp, he said, when he was driving the cows, some cows went astray in the bushes, so he put her on path and went to bring the cows out of thick thorny trees, returning, he never found Achol. The rich man got annoyed but he forgave him. Keny continued to keep his cattle, after the loss of Achol.

In the forest that day, Achol had, , been crying and crying, more and more, calling out, "Mama, Mama, Mama," and there was no Mother or anyone to answer her call. Achol kept on moving alone in the forest until the night fell. Through half of the night, Achol walked and walked, cried and cried again and again, calling out, "Mama, Mama, Mama,' until she sat down and fell asleep. In the morning she woke up and she continued wandering and crying. She was crying in the lowest and most hoarse voice, because of crying for so long. Finally, the Creator heard her crying and the female Lion heard her voice and she came, answering.

"Yes my child?"

The Lion Mother had picked up Achol, kissing its mouth but Achol shook her head and she said: "Your mouth smells and doesn't smell like my Mother's mouth." The Lion didn't care about what Achol was saying and she carried her home. She removed all the thorns on her feet.

In morning, the Lion Mother went into the forest and she caught a reedbuck, she milked her and she brought the milk to Achol. In following morning, the Lion Mother, chased and caught an antelope, milked her, and she brought the milk to Achol.

For a long space of time the Lion Mother had been feeding Achol with milk of the animals until she had grown up, and she began to eat food. Achol became a very big girl at the Lion's home. She was then a Lion's daughter.

The Lion made a bed with the longest poles, without climbing-steps on the pole. When she was about to go hunting, the Lion would say to Achol, "Achol close your eyes." Then Achol would close her eyes, and the Lion tied steps upon the pole, and she carried Achol up to the bed, she removed the steps, then hid them. Then she said, "Achol, open your eyes." Achol opened her eyes. The Lion had been putting Achol up on the bed because if she left her down, the other man-eaters might eat her.

One afternoon, a man called Deng was searching for his lost cows. He came acoss the Lion's home. He saw a beautiful girl sitting up on a tall-legged bed without climbing-steps on it. He came under the bed,greeting the girl and the girl greeted him too. He asked the girl's name, the girl said she is Achol. He asked how she got up there, Achol said that she didn't know how she got up because she is always being told to close her eyes every day, then she is taken up by her Mother.

Deng asked Achol where her Mother was. Achol said her Mother had gone hunting. She promised him that in the following morning, she would have to look at how the Lion her Mother would take her up to the bed. Then Deng left.

In the evening the Lion came, and she brought Achol down as usual. "Achol, close your eyes." She closed her eyes half-way. As the Lion was tying the steps on the legs of the bed, Achol was secretly looking through the fingers of her hands. The Lion brought Achol down. They slept. In the following morning, the Lion said, "Achol, close your eyes." She closed her eyes half-way, looking through the fingers of her hands, at how the Lion had been tying the steps, removing them and where she had hidden them.

As soon as the Lion had gone, Deng came. Achol showed him where the Lion had hidden the steps. Deng took the steps and he tied the steps, and Achol came down. Achol and Deng talked happily and lovingly for the whole day. When it was a time the Lion was about to come, Deng tied the steps and Achol climbed up to the bed and he hid the steps in the place the Lion had hidden them and he left.

The Lion came and she said "Achol, close your eyes," Achol closed her eyes and the Lion brought her down. In the evening, the Lion put Achol in her house

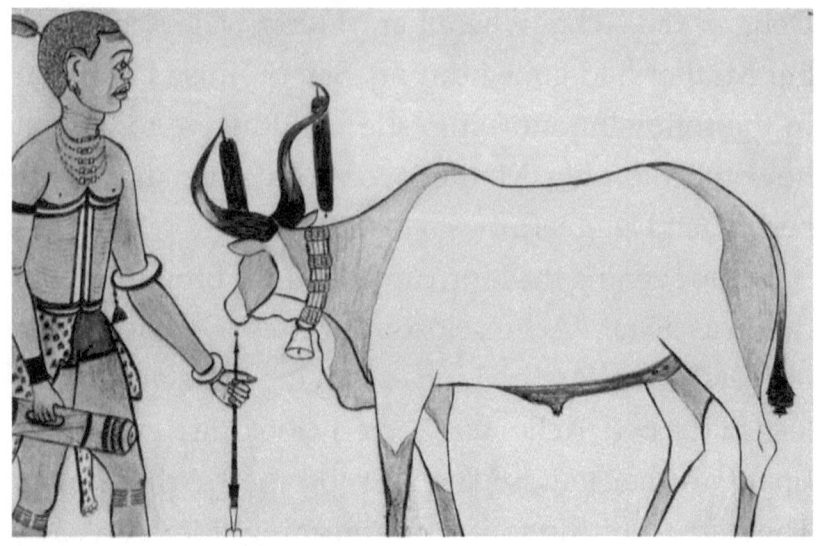

and locked her door with big wood as usual. After, the Lion entered her own house.

Deng came back at night and he opened the door of Achol and he entered the house. They started to talk slowly. The Lion heard their voices. The Lion came and asked "Achol, who is talking with you?"

"No one, my Mother, I am the one singing alone," said Achol.

In a short space of time, the Lion fell sleep. Achol came out and she looked at her, she saw her tail has already crept out. When the man-eater Lion is awoken, it has no tail and if it sleeps, its tail creeps out.

At that time, Achol and Deng left for the human being's home. They walked at night until they reached Deng's home in the morning. Deng told his Father and Mother that he brought his wife. His parents saw Achol and she was extremely beautiful and they were pleased with her.

In the morning, when the Lion woke up, she never found Achol. The Lion broke in tears, she cried, she danced angrily more and more. She sang the song;

My daughter, Achol
Whom I brought up
With milk of reedbucks, giraffes
Where has she gone?

My daughter, Achol
Whom I brought up
With meat of antelope, waterbuck
Where has she gone?

My daughter, Achol
Whom I brought up
With sorghum of my arm
Where has she gone?

Oh Creator,
Help me
To get Achol!

After she finished dancing, crying and singing, she took *cuoc*, a twisted circle head pad, and she threw it onto the path that, leads to where the sun rises. It returned back and she threw it to the path leading to where the sun sets. It returned, she threw it onto a path to the left, the *cuoc* ran straight to the left, the Lion followed it. The *cuoc* was running and rolling in front and the Lion was following it until it arrived at Deng's home, entering where Achol was sitting, and it stopped on Achol's lap. The Lion entered the house, too. She saw Achol inside, she pulled her out, and left with her. The parents of Deng stopped the Lion from taking Achol. The Lion said Achol was her daughter, so they entered into a talk of marriage. The Lion agreed to the marriage and she asked for 30 bulls. She drove her bulls to her village.

In the following night, Deng and his wife Achol went to sleep in the house. At night, Deng wanted to sleep with Achol but the papyrus mat, which they were sleeping on, sang a song:

> *Do not touch her*
> *She is your sister*
> *Do not touch her*
> *She is the last born*
> *of your Mother.*

Deng was surprised and he stopped to sleep with her that night. On the second night, Deng came and wanted to sleep with Achol, the papyrus sang the same song. Deng stopped and he slept alone.

In the morning, Deng told his uncle about the song, the papyrus had been singing to him at night when he wanted to sleep with his wife. In the night, the uncle came and hid near the house. When Deng wanted to sleep with Achol, the papyrus sang the song. His uncle came over and he said, "You leave her, I heard the song."

During the day, his uncle called his brother, the Father of Deng and they went and brought the Magician. The song was explained to the Magician. The Magician said, "Achol is your daughter, who was lost in the forest by your servant Keny." When the parents of Deng heard this news, they cried and cried.

The Father of Achol and Deng brought a bull, and it was sacrificed on the papyrus mat. The meat of the sacrificial animal was not eaten; it was thrown away. Another bull was speared for the celebration. After a few days, Achol was married by another man with many cows. Deng married his wife by the bridewealth of Achol.

www.ingramcontent.com/pod-product-compliance
Lightning Source LLC
Chambersburg PA
CBHW020513120726
47904CB00003B/819